# PROM
# HOUSE

# PROM HOUSE

## CHELSEA MUELLER

*Underlined*

Text copyright © 2021 by Chelsea Mueller
Cover art copyright © 2021 by kid-ethic
Cover art used under license from Shutterstock.com
Beach house copyright © 2021 by Oleg Albinsky/Getty Images

All rights reserved. Published in the United States by Underlined,
an imprint of Random House Children's Books, a division
of Penguin Random House LLC, New York.

Underlined is a registered trademark and the colophon is a trademark
of Penguin Random House LLC.

GetUnderlined.com

Educators and librarians, for a variety of teaching tools,
visit us at RHTeachersLibrarians.com

*Library of Congress Cataloging-in-Publication Data*
Names: Mueller, Chelsea, author.
Title: Prom house / Chelsea Mueller.
Description: First edition. | New York : Underlined, [2021] | Audience: Ages 12
and up | Summary: "Ten people are invited to share a prom house at the
Jersey Shore for the weekend. Every one of them has a secret . . . and when
one by one they begin to die, panic ensues. Could somebody's prom date
also be . . . a killer?"—Provided by publisher.
Identifiers: LCCN 2020026012 (print) | LCCN 2020026013 (ebook) |
ISBN 978-0-593-18005-1 (trade paperback) | ISBN 978-0-593-18006-8 (ebook)
Subjects: CYAC: Horror stories. | Murder—Fiction. | Secrets—Fiction. |
Parties—Fiction. | Friendship—Fiction.
Classification: LCC PZ7.1.M75 Pr 2021 (print) | LCC PZ7.1.M75 (ebook) |
DDC [Fic]—dc23

The text of this book is set in 10.75-point Times New Roman MT Std.
Interior design by Jen Valero

Printed in the United States of America
10 9 8 7 6 5 4 3 2 1
First Edition

# PROM
# HOUSE

# one

I WAS *not* prepared for a house this swanky. As I stood outside on the wide, wraparound porch, I couldn't help but gape
at the glamorous dark paneling and white trim. Rentals—
*especially* party rentals—usually came with shabby carpet and
dripping refrigerators. Judging by the exterior, this Jersey Shore
mansion was none of that. It was movie-level luxe, and I was
staying here with my friends for an epic prom weekend.

"Yes!" I whispered.

My best friend, Aubrey, who had been standing shoulder to
shoulder with me, opened the door without knocking. I stepped
forward to catch the door before it closed behind her, the porch
planks creaking in my wake. Crisp, cold landscaping lights shot
up from behind the green bushes, illuminating the commanding white columns at the front of the three-story house.

"Kylie, you coming?" Aubrey had both hands wrapped
around the crossbody strap of her overnight bag, like her
clothes were about to make a break for the beach.

I shrugged my considerably lighter bag higher on my shoulder and walked inside. "This place is ridiculous."

"Right?" Even in the low light of the huge foyer, I could see that Aubrey was beaming. Her auburn hair was pulled tight into a perfect ballerina bun, but she sauntered toward the living room with the grace of a newborn giraffe.

"Watch the—"

The tip of her shoe snagged on the rug, and she pitched forward. The sofa caught her before I could.

"Rug?" Her laugh was clear and high. Nothing was going to ruin this weekend for her.

I needed to get in the same mindset, even if this plush furniture and the wildly ornate candlesticks sitting on the mantel above an oversized fireplace made me feel even more out of place. My house had a standard stoop, not this wraparound porch fanciness.

"Who rents out a party house and leaves so much breakable stuff?" *Overly trusting adults,* I guessed.

Aubrey shrugged. "People who have money to burn."

"People ready to make a quick ten grand off seniors." Aubrey's boyfriend, Cam, sauntered into the house behind me. He let out a low whistle at the interior.

"You mean like ten *thousand* dollars?" Even saying that number aloud made my throat squeeze.

"Wait, so Kylie didn't front the cash?" Cam didn't bother disguising his sneer. He'd buzzed his hair a couple weeks ago, and it somehow made him look meaner.

Aubrey planted a fist on her hip. "Don't be a dick."

"What? I'm kidding." He rolled his head from side to side, like he was preparing for a fight. "Kylie, the house is covered. Don't freak."

"That's not an apology," Aubrey muttered.

This was supposed to be our first weekend of freedom. But within seconds of stepping inside this incredible party house, Cam and Aubrey were already sniping at each other.

"Babe."

"Don't *babe* me."

He shuffled closer to her. His shoes screeched against the hardwood floor. "Let it go, Aub. You wanted to do this."

He cradled her face in the palm of his hand, and I had to look away. This is what they did. A fire-and-ice routine that left her crying every other weekend. Jabbing at each other until he made promises he wouldn't keep. I started toward the stairs. Aubrey's pouty "I wanted to have the prom you promised me" followed me, but I didn't look back to see if she was caving to his dimples.

This rental was the most secluded house I'd ever seen on the Jersey Shore. We were out on the end of a long road and right up next to the beach. Which was great, knowing how loud we could get when we partied, but I wasn't supposed to be alone here with just Cam and Aubrey for company. Especially not when they were already going at it.

"Liam? Holli? Rory?" I started shouting my other friends' names to see who might call back. A precursor to the round of Marco Polo we'd most likely play in the pool after we got back from the dance.

"Noah told me he's already here. He's probably staked out primo digs upstairs." Cam's voice was raspy behind me. I turned and found him and Aubrey standing at the bottom of the stairs; Aubrey's cheeks were heated. *That resolved itself quickly.* She pulled her phone from the front pocket of her oversize week-ender. A swipe and a trio of taps later, she announced, "Dani and Hudson are already here somewhere, too. Rory is stuck in traffic, and everyone else is in her car."

"Everyone?" The tightness in my chest tried to strangle the word. Seven of our friends were joining us for the weekend: Noah, Dani, Hudson, Rory, Holli, Vic, and . . .

Aubrey got a dimple in her cheek when she smiled. "Even Liam."

"Oh, good." Though I could tell my cheeks were burning, Aubrey didn't call me out. Liam was my boyfriend, but we hadn't been dating long, and I knew clingy wasn't a good look. "He thought he'd be here first."

Aubrey darted past me. "Did anyone call dibs on rooms beforehand?"

"This is a finders, keepers situation, Aub." And the sooner I found a room to claim, the sooner I could distract myself with prom prep. I was banking on Aubrey pinning my deep brown hair into a prom-worthy updo. She'd brought the flat iron for some 1920s-style finger waves but promised she wasn't going to burn my ear again. Third time's the charm, right?

And speaking of prom-worthy, I couldn't believe I'd landed my dream date. Liam and I had had classes together for years, but we'd only started dating a month ago. I almost hadn't recognized him after winter break; he'd grown what seemed like six inches. When he leaned forward with that messy black hair flopping over his green eyes, I went gooey. All languid limbs, bands of tension snapping up from my hips to my chest, and rushes of effervescent bubbles to my brain. Every. Single. Time.

I wasn't sure I was prepared for how he was going to look in a tuxedo. Or how I was going to handle being with him in this house. Aubrey had made me pack the skimpiest swimsuit

I owned, and I was already cringing at the thought of poolside wardrobe malfunctions. Not to mention the more pervasive mental image of me purposefully pulling the string on the back of my bikini because I wanted to show Liam more. *Did I?*

The first room we passed had two twin beds pushed up against opposite walls. A desk with a stack of leather-bound books was wedged beneath a windowsill.

Aubrey didn't even pause. "Pass."

Cam grumbled behind me. "It's just a place to crash for a couple nights."

The hallway pivoted right. For a tall, square house, the interior was oddly serpentine. The next door we passed was closed. I gripped the brass knob, but before I could twist it, a high-pitched squeak slipped out. I flinched, then realized the sound was coming from inside the room. There was another squeak, and another. *Bedsprings.* I peeled my fingers away from the knob before I alerted the couple on the other side.

Aubrey's eyes widened.

I mouthed, "Found Hudson and Dani."

Cam simply smirked. "A bed's a bed, ladies."

Aubrey and I had to scurry down the hall with our hands clasped over our mouths to keep the laughter from spilling out.

Safely up on the third floor, we found bedrooms across the hall from one another, and a bathroom between them that was big enough for prom prep.

"We each get a room?" I still couldn't believe it.

"I know how you are. Told everyone we needed megaspace for maximum cuteness," Aubrey said.

The four-poster bed in my room was enormous. Five people could sleep in this bed. I mean, they wouldn't, but the *space.* As

I was reveling in its sheer size, Aubrey slipped into the room. She'd ditched her shoes, and her toenails were painted a posy pink. I toed off my own canvas sneakers. She nodded at my riotous lime-green polish. "Niiiiice."

"Cam settling in?" He hadn't followed her.

"Said he needed to 'set up' for the party." She rolled her eyes, which meant he had to be toting in coolers of beer.

I dove onto the bed, landing starfish style at the center. The mattress threatened to swallow me in downy softness.

"I still can't believe my mom went for this," I said to the textured ceiling, refusing to let Cam and Aubrey's relationship drama ruin prom prep.

Aubrey flopped down next to me on the bed. "She knew I'd be a good influence."

I rolled my eyes at her. "She said it was about proving I was a responsible young adult." I tried to mimic my mom's serious voice, all stoic and concerned.

"I just told mine I was rooming with you." Aubrey tapped her heels against the footboard.

Even when I stretched, my toes barely made it to the wood at the end of the bed. Would Liam fit? His feet had dangled off the edge of my bed at home, but he hadn't slept over, so it didn't matter.

No, I chided myself, I wasn't going to think about what might happen in this bed tonight. I was going to focus on getting ready for prom. My ears burned anyway. Stupid brain.

"It probably helped that Liam and I are such a new thing. I mean, he's thoughtful and my mom likes him." When I said our names together, the words had this umami tang, like I was testing a new flavor. Maybe Mom thought I wouldn't rush into anything serious with Liam, the same way I refused to choose a mom-approved dress for graduation. The difference was I *liked* the way Liam felt against me, unlike all of those scratchy dresses.

"Yeah. Wouldn't have worked with my mom."

"It's not like you and Cam are new," I countered.

"Well, he does sneak out of my house at least once a week." Pink splotches dappled the sides of her neck. New or not, grumpy or not, Cam was it for Aubrey. "And calling it sneaking is generous. He's so bulky. I love it, but he's even less coordinated than me."

A door slammed somewhere downstairs, followed by a flurry of muffled voices that shook me from my thoughts. This weekend wasn't about sneaking. I wouldn't have to hide my beer, I wouldn't have to hold back with Liam if I didn't want to, and I wouldn't have to worry about steering clear of drama. It was prom weekend, and we had super-fancy digs. Tonight was going to be one hell of a rager.

# two

OLD HOUSES weren't built for the power of well-placed Bluetooth speakers. Our rental offered speakers on the back patio, but Liam and his best friend, Noah, had brought their own to augment the audio. Every wall in the five-bedroom home carried the slapping bass line of whatever current bop was blasting outdoors. We'd only been back from prom for a couple hours, and already our party was perfection.

Liam's hand slipped around my back to rest low on my hip. Heat bubbled beneath my breastbone, and it had zero to do with the second bottle of sparkling wine I'd split with Rory and Aubrey. Tendrils of hair fell around my face and tickled the nape of my neck; Aubrey hadn't burned me once in preparing the perfect 1920s updo, but her pin job might need work.

"You really do look gorgeous tonight, K." Liam's lips brushed my ear, and I shivered.

He looked like a dark-haired Hemsworth brother. His tie hung loose, and he'd unbuttoned the top of his white shirt. The rest of him was still tailored, though. His shirt was tucked in, which highlighted his trim waist and made his shoulders look ten times broader. As my eyes raked over him, the corner of his mouth quirked up. Oh, man. I was staring. I jerked my gaze away, landing instead on the coolers lining the concrete patio that were brimming with bottles of beer, wine, and someone's dad's whiskey.

I pretended I could hear the crashing of the nearby ocean waves over the splashing in the pool and the music and the rumble of voices, but really I was tuned in to the sound of Liam's heartbeat, fast but steady. I looked back at him for a half second. His eyes were shuttered, but that pounding pulse was visible in the side of his neck. My own heartbeat threatened to choke me. Was there a move I needed to make now? It was too dark to see the shore—just the horizon disappearing into blackness—but I watched like I would find someone who could tell me what I was supposed to do next. I'd spent the last month trying not to be overeager, but when he looked like this? I didn't stand a chance.

Noah clapped a hand against Liam's back, hard enough to jostle me. He towered at six feet tall, but with his long dirty-blond hair whipped into a bun at the nape of his neck and his slim, slouched frame, Noah looked almost scrawny. "You ready to do this?"

The gleam in his eye should have worried me. Nothing good came from impish smiles and mischievous delight when Noah was involved.

Liam dropped his arm from my hip, and I sucked in a couple steadying breaths. That tiny bit of distance allowed me to come to my senses. His touch did something to me, something thrilling and kind of terrifying.

"Oh hell yes," Liam said to his friend. To me, he added, "Back in five. Keep an eye out. You're going to love this."

I gave him my signature skeptical glance. "Impress me," I said with confidence I didn't own, still thinking about the way his fingers had skimmed my skin.

He planted a quick kiss on my forehead and disappeared into the house with Noah.

Lights placed beneath the water set the pool ablaze with a cerulean-green glow. It was enough to make it more tropics and less Shore. A string of fairy lights over the patio swayed in the gusty wind. I sat at the edge and let my feet dangle in the warm water.

Rory swam up to me, her round face framed by slicked-back pool hair. Rory had been the third member of our friendship power triangle since sixth grade. She'd pulled the bobby pins from her short, dark hair and cannonballed into the pool within five minutes of returning from prom. She lifted her chin toward me, and the rebellious gleam in her eyes blazed. "I don't know who picked this place, but *baller.*"

I wasn't sure who had found this place either. Aubrey and Liam both had invites and told me I didn't need to drop cash for the room. Should I have asked more questions? I looked at the rap-video setup we had for this backyard—the bottles of booze resting poolside, the pristine white lounge chairs, the gold and green glowing lights pressing up from the water and down from the eaves of the house. *Nah.*

"Holy . . . Isn't that your boyfriend?" Rory pointed behind me. No, *above* me.

I turned and found Liam perched at the edge of the second-story roof. Noah was clambering out of a windowsill a few feet away. My stomach sank. Was this supposed to be impressive?

It'd started to rain. Not enough to dampen our party, but the shingles of the roof overhead shimmered like submerged slate.

"No diving board is no fun," Noah shouted.

Hudson, his dark skin warming beneath the string lights overhead, ignored him. If we hadn't scored this rental, Hudson would have thrown a party of his own. "Hey, Dani," he shouted before chucking an inflatable beach ball at his girlfriend's head with a precision that proved why he'd earned a lacrosse scholarship. She splashed him, but turned her attention to the guys on the roof before she could see him shake the water from his short, coiled Mohawk.

"You've got to be kidding." Holli, a Florida girl who had adjusted to New Jersey life faster than I would have, swiped a hand over her pink curls.

Noah wasn't kidding. Hudson and Dani started heckling the guys, and quickly Rory and even Aubrey started cheering them on. I didn't see Vic or Cam, but Noah didn't need their encouragement.

Noah smirked. "We make our own fun."

Liam rose out of a crouch and *good God.* He'd ditched his shirt and his pants. I hadn't seen him out of his pants before, and those boxer briefs left very little to the imagination. Every inch of his tanned skin was taut, his muscles locked and eager to move, and deep lines carved a sharp V at his hips. I looked back at the water, as if it might cool the fire flashing to my cheeks and loosen the knot forming in my stomach.

"Kylie!" he called. His smile pulled wide into a full-on grin. "Comin' for you, babe."

He leaped. It wasn't a sexy swimmer dive. It was a power jump from a swath of shingles, but he landed with a proper splash, and the wake crashed over my head. My hair was plastered to my face, Aubrey's careful crimping gone in an instant. I swiped the soaked locks back to a chorus of laughter. I could only smile and shake my head. This boy was trouble.

Noah followed him swiftly, and the two lazily treaded water, cracking jokes that didn't reach my ears.

Aubrey sat next to me, her ankle knocking against mine in the illuminated water. Despite the playful nudge, her mouth was pulled tight. "Have you seen Cam?"

"Not in a bit. Figured he was off getting you a drink," I said. I didn't want to admit I'd been wrapped up in my own nerves.

Aubrey lifted her half-full plastic wineglass.

Rory propped her elbows on the pool's edge. The shoulder straps of her black swimsuit cut into her olive skin. "I saw him maybe an hour ago getting beer."

Aubrey folded her arms across her chest, a barricade to keep her worries in and the panic out. She flicked her gaze over to Dani. Both she and Hudson had climbed out of the pool, but the light rain hadn't ushered them under the house's eaves. Dani's long black hair was slicked down her back. She whispered in Hudson's ear, but when she pulled back, her lips were in a tight pout.

"I haven't seen Vic in a minute either—"

"You say that like it's a bad thing." Rory didn't bother hiding her dislike for Vic, the junior Noah had brought as his plus-one to our party.

Lightning flickered over the ocean. Waves crested beneath the flash of the faraway storm. "The storm better not crash this party," I said.

Rory grinned. "A little rain hasn't hurt us so far."

Aubrey's fingers fluttered against her upper arms.

"Do you think Cam went upstairs?" I asked, reading my best friend's worry.

She dropped her hands back to her sides. "Maybe."

I tilted my chin toward the pool and my boyfriend, the one I'd yet to decide what I wanted to do with tonight. I needed more time. "He's not getting out of there any time soon. Let's go find Cam."

Holli watched us closely from her perch on the other edge of the pool. Rory smiled at her, and dimples appeared in her round cheeks.

"You guys go ahead without me," Rory said as she swam off toward her girlfriend. It was probably for the best. Rory's lack of filter meant Aubrey would only get angrier about her current dude drama.

Liam was still in the pool, laughing at his rooftop antics with Noah. Aubrey bumped her shoulder against mine, and we went in search of her boyfriend.

The oak floors inside the house vibrated with the beat of our music. Props to prom house placement that no one had called the cops on us yet. The massive, five-bedroom house was bright—stainless steel in the kitchen, polished granite in the bathrooms, flat screens at every turn. The rental was filled with perks, but no sign of Cam.

The lounge chairs on the pool deck were empty, the umbrellas over the outdoor tables tilted beneath a steady wind, but our party raged on. I spotted Vic leaning over the side of the pool near Holli and Rory. His full lips were pulled back in a sneer. From the tight pull of Holli's pink lips, he wasn't saying anything nice. Vic had the charm of a brick and still tried to hit on every girl he met, regardless of their relationship status or orientation.

Aubrey and I waved off offers to jump back into the water and continued looking for her boyfriend. The gate to the white fence surrounding the pool unlatched easily, and small, bright lights guided us along the wooden deck path that wound around the side of the house.

Two outdoor showers were hidden by a small partition at the back of the house. "He couldn't be in there, right?"

Aubrey paled but leaned forward to check for feet beneath the wood. "No one in there."

"Of course not," I said, probably too quickly. It was a testament to how solid the pool party was that no one had snuck away to make out there.

Even on a property this large, there were only so many places to look. Tucked behind the home, beyond the pool, was a stone firepit.

That is where we found Cam.

The cool, blue landscaping lights buried behind the bushes stopped at the edge of the deck. I stepped down onto a sandy path. Smoke filled my sinuses, blocking out all other scents.

We saw his feet first. He'd kicked off his shoes, but granules of sand clung to his heels. Brown and green glass shards littered the edges of the pit. He was stretched out on his side, his chest close to the flagstones enclosing the dying fire. His head was haloed in broken glass.

He wasn't moving.

Aubrey ran to him. Called his name. He didn't stir.

"Aub, the glass!" I shouted.

She ignored me. The ground was darker near Cam. She shook him, but he didn't respond.

I tiptoed closer as quickly as I could without slicing open my feet. Someone would need to run for help if he'd drunk too much again.

Aubrey let out a sharp cry, like the keening of a widow calling out to sea. When I reached her, I saw why.

Cam's glazed eyes looked up sightlessly at the blackened sky. The logs smoldering in the firepit flickered orange and yellow over his unmoving chest. Blood sluiced down beneath his starched shirt from the fist-sized glass shard that was buried in Cam's neck.

Cam was dead.

# three

ANOTHER SHARP scream pierced the air. My throat was squeezed far too tight to make a single sound in response. Rivulets of panic dripped along each of my ribs until my chest was alight with the ache of anxiety. The crashing of waves was swallowed by the plaintive bellow.

Finally the scream shuttered and was replaced with heavy, gasping breaths. I turned on rubber legs to find Rory, hand clasped to her mouth, her round face pulled gaunt by the horror at my feet.

I staggered away from Cam. *He* wasn't crying out. Blood oozed from his wounds. The rain made the blood appear to flow faster.

Aubrey was still kneeling at his side. She looked up at me like I was supposed to know what to do next, tears gleaming in the low firelight. But my whole body felt numb. All I'd expected from this weekend was some alone time with Liam and a quality party. This was my first dead body, and I 100 percent did not know what to do.

"W-w-we should call nine-one-one," I managed to say.

I patted my bikini like my phone would magically appear. I shook myself—or was that shock setting in? Our phones were inside, charging.

Had we really been draped in silk and chiffon dancing to overplayed pop hits only hours ago?

*Crap crap crap.* I stumbled backward, away from Cam, from the body, from the *crime scene.* I fell to the sandy earth. Something sharp bit my hand. I plucked a fleck of glass, no bigger than my pinkie, from my palm.

Neither of my friends moved to help me up. I wasn't sure I could stand anyway.

"What happened?" The sea threatened to steal Rory's words, but the grave note in her voice anchored them.

"He's gone." Aubrey's shoulders shook, her hoop earrings swaying with the movement.

Rory crept closer, but stopped at the outer edge of the broken glass. There was more of it than I'd realized. At least a half dozen bottles had been shattered, and more than just the brown and green glass of beer bottles. I recognized a whiskey label and another from the tequila Vic swore his dad wouldn't miss.

"Was Cam drinking alone again?" Rory asked, like it hadn't been a secret. Aubrey had only told us because she'd broken up with Cam twice after he'd ditched her at parties to down a fifth of *whatever.*

Aubrey recoiled. She pressed a hand to Cam's chest absentmindedly, then snatched it back like it was a hot cooktop.

"Pretty sure he couldn't have been drunk enough to kill himself." The stark truth of the sight made me speak bluntly.

"It could have been an accident," Rory countered.

I pushed up from the ground. "No one accidentally stabs themselves in the neck."

Aubrey began crying in earnest. Both Rory and I muttered apologies. Standing here wasn't going to fix this. Could we fix this?

Lightning flashed over the water to my right, and the heavy crack of thunder rang a moment later.

"Who would want to kill Cam?" I hadn't meant to say the words aloud, but the truth of what lay before us demanded it.

"This isn't real. This *can't* be real." Aubrey tucked her chin to her chest, like she could block out the truth.

Rory sidled closer to me. "He's really dead, isn't he?"

I nodded.

Rory gripped my upper arm, her nails claiming purchase. "We shouldn't be out here."

The music from the poolside speakers was barely a muffled rumble here. The bushes and fencing were for more than style points, I guessed—it was an extremely secluded spot. I cast a look back to the warm green and golden glow above the pool. No one else had come out after us.

"You're right." Fear scraped my throat, and the salty air made my eyes well with tears. Cam couldn't have been out here long. He was still *bleeding.* I managed a hoarse whisper. "Whoever did this could still be out here."

Rory yanked me close. Her shoulder knocked mine. "You think he's watching us?"

"He already killed Cam. What more could he do?" Aubrey said between hiccupping breaths.

I wasn't going to answer that. If Aubrey's mind wasn't already spinning a trillion scenarios from slasher films, I wasn't about to shove them into her brain.

"C'mon, Aub." I tried for my most reasonable friend voice and was pretty certain she couldn't hear my panic. "Rory's right. We shouldn't be out here. Whoever did this could be on the beach. We need to get inside and call the cops."

I extended my free hand to Aubrey. She didn't take it.

Rory had none of my chill. "Everyone's down the Shore this weekend. The killer could be next door."

Or in the house. Had Cam actually been out here alone? Could someone in our own house have done this? Could one of our friends have killed Cam?

Just then, abrupt silence cut into the night.

The house went dark. The tropical glow of a shoreside pool was doused, and the muffled music shut off.

Rory wasn't the only one who screamed this time.

# four

AS WE huddled in the eerie quiet, a dark shadow crept toward us from the house. The darkness was long and broad and moving too fast.

I froze. *The killer.*

He'd heard us. He was coming back to finish us off.

"You guys okay?" Liam's shout was like a punch to my solar plexus. I gasped out a breath of relief, even as my mouth went dry with fear. Liam didn't know there was a killer nearby, and he was strolling around in the dark like an idiot.

"C-C-Cam . . ." Aubrey managed to eke out her boyfriend's name.

Liam strode forward like she hadn't spoken. His face came into view in the gentle firelight, that sharp jawline ready to cut through my defenses.

"Noah tripped the circuit breaker," he said. "Tunes will be back *un momento.*"

"Liam."

It might have been the mangled sound of his name from my lips or the choked sob from Aubrey that forced Liam to look down. He stopped short, his sandal slipping off his foot. His mouth opened, but he didn't wail like Rory and he didn't cry like Aubrey. Instead, he looked completely lost—just like me.

With a sudden ferocity, I wished I could rewind the night. Go back to Liam in his shiny black tux and my hands up around his neck . . .

*It had taken me three shopping trips to find this dress. Intricate beads woven over mesh cascaded down a deep V-neck into an open A-line tulle skirt with a slit that showed skin at just the right times. It was weightless and luxurious at the same time, but it was the color that had hooked me. The delicate merging of cotton candy and starlight. I'd tried to re-create the color in a vase I made for Mother's Day, but even with the fine-grained porcelain, the feel wasn't quite right.*

*This dress, though? Liam looking at me like I was the only person at the dance? Definitely right.*

*"I can almost pretend we're alone." Liam's laugh was husky at my ear. A shiver teased my spine.*

*I shrugged to cover it, and the act only drew me closer to him. "That's because Dani and Hudson have already disappeared."*

*Our most athletic friends were a hot couple. They'd also climbed on top of each other at every opportunity for the last six months. A little flare ignited in my chest. Did Liam and I look like that now?*

*Liam skimmed his hand over my lower back, and he smiled wide. "They overestimate how much coverage the cardboard trees provide. Mr. Simpson is going to bust them in three . . . two . . . one."*

*Sure enough, the freshman social studies teacher yanked Hudson out by the arm. I hadn't thought Simpson was strong enough to overwhelm the bulky lacrosse starter, but when Dani followed him, cleaning her smudged maroon lipstick with her thumb, it was clear why he'd been caught off guard.*

*"Mind if I cut in?" Noah tried to slip his elbow between us.*

*"Not a chance," Liam said, knocking his best friend back a step.*

*Noah's tux was the same shiny black as Liam's, but the inseam was an inch too short—or his legs were too long. He slouched and edged closer, like he was joining us in our slow dance.*

*"I know your mom taught you to share." The light lilt in Noah's voice didn't stop me from rolling my eyes.*

*"You don't share people," I muttered.*

*Before Noah could reply, Liam said, "You said you wanted to go stag. Enjoy it, man."*

*"So I could dance with anyone." Noah's laugh was tight. I wasn't supposed to know, but Noah was going to get another chance at senior prom next year; Liam told me he'd failed out and had to repeat twelfth grade. Maybe that's why he'd brought his obnoxious friend, a junior named Vic, as his plus-one to the party.*

*"You guys ready to ditch this place?" Aubrey was glued to Cam's side. A flush stretched beneath his close-cropped blond hair. His eyes, though, were marking the exits.*

*"Thought the whole night was about prom," I said. Why was she in such a hurry to leave the dance?*

*"Prom is the pretext for the party." She shook her head like this was standard procedure. It probably was, but I actually had a boyfriend this year, i.e., an excuse to wrap my arms around a super-hot guy.*

*"One more song," Liam offered.*

*Aubrey cast a glance to Rory, who was splitting a chair with her girlfriend, Holli, and ignoring the mass of bodies on the dance floor. Rory's olive skin warmed against the emerald fabric she teased at Holli's knee.*

*Liam's hand slipped low enough on my back that his finger-tips skimmed my butt. I swallowed hard, thankful for the heavy bass pulsing throughout the hall. "Just one more."*

We should have stayed at the dance. Cam couldn't have disappeared there. We wouldn't be standing in sand sifted with blood and glass. We wouldn't have to explain this.

"What happened?" Liam's voice was low with horror.

Rory took a couple steps toward the house. She slathered sass over her words, like we wouldn't see her shaking hands and wide eyes. Like it would stave off the fear. "If we knew, do you think we'd be standing here with bloody feet?"

Liam kneeled next to Cam. He tilted Cam's chin to the side, the moonlight and firelight warring over the bloody column of his neck. Aubrey's brows furrowed, but she didn't bristle. Fresh blood oozed from around the glass.

"Don't touch it," I said before he could put his fingers on the shard.

"I wasn't going to," Liam snapped over his shoulder. His green eyes were almost black out here. Raindrops speckled his cheeks. The charming facade of the guy who'd hopped off the roof was replaced with this harsh version looming over his friend.

I didn't back away at his hardened glare.

"Sorry." He swiped a hand across his mouth, and then edged away from the body. "How could this have happened?"

He stood next to me, and I let him take my hand. His fingers were damp, and my stomach flipped. *It's not blood. It's not blood.*

He leaned his shoulder against mine, and I was steadier.

"I get the booze, but how did that . . ." He trailed off, unready or unwilling to describe the sight before us.

Aubrey clung to Cam's hand and muttered, "I need to call his mom" over and over. Her voice was barely a whisper.

There was a sharp crack and a heavy crash from out in the bramble. Liam yanked me closer. His heart was racing, but his voice was firm. "Did you call the cops?"

I shook my head. "Our phones are on the charging pad on the patio." I said it like it was an excuse. I didn't need a reason, but the realization that I was standing in a crime scene made me want an alibi.

Liam's camo board shorts had pockets. Of course they did. He pulled his phone out but didn't immediately dial. His hands were shaking. He stared at his friend—he'd known Cam far better than I had, far better than he knew me—and his throat bobbed.

He swiped over to the emergency button.

The call rang out between us. The slosh of the sea had softened, like even the ocean was holding its breath.

"Nine-one-one, what's your emergency?" The stern male voice was loud enough for us all to hear, even with the phone pressed to Liam's ear.

"I—I need to report . . . ," Liam stuttered.

"Just tell them!" Rory shouted. The hard glint to her words would have packed a harder punch if her eyes weren't ringed in red.

"What's your emergency?" the 911 operator repeated, more forcefully this time.

"I need to report a murder."

There was a pause just long enough to feel like the operator had hung up. "What's your location?"

"We're at a Shore house." Liam's eyes widened. He cupped a hand over the phone and whispered, "Does anyone remember the address here?"

"Sir, can you tell me where you are?" There was a note of urgency in the operator's voice.

Liam scrambled. "We're out back behind the house. I don't know the address. It's big and white and at the end of a cul-de-sac."

Those were toddler directions. We needed to do better. I told Liam the street name, but I had no idea what the house number was. He relayed the information to the man on the other end of the line.

"What happened exactly?"

Liam's hardened gaze fell on Cam's bloody throat. "Our friend was murdered. That's what happened. We need you to send someone."

"Look, kid, you're the seventeenth call tonight that has been about an emergency at the Shore. Death, destruction, kidnapping. Every report has been fake."

"He's really dead," Liam sputtered.

The panic prickling my chest was scalded by my anger. We called for help and they're calling us liars. We were stuck here, with no idea what to do next other than ask for help and they had the audacity to say this was a prank?

No. Aubrey was broken, my insides were barely solid, Liam

was in shock, and Cam? Cam was dead. We needed help, and I was going to get it.

I extended a hand toward his phone. "Can I?"

He acquiesced.

"Listen, my friend is dead." The words rushed out in a blazing march. "You have to take this seriously. Okay? We need help."

Our friend was dead.

At our bare feet.

The emergency operator sighed and asked a series of questions about Cam's status, about where we were. With each question, there was a new layer of weariness in the operator's voice.

"So your friend has been stabbed outside of a beach house and there are how many people on-site?"

I was done with this questioning. Seriously, how many jerks prank-called 911? "Are you sending someone?"

There was a long pause.

"We need someone. *He* needs someone. Whoever did this could still be here." Fear lapped at my indignation.

Finally, the operator said, "Officers have been dispatched to your location."

"What do we do until then? Ask him," Rory half whispered.

I repeated her question.

"Go inside, lock the doors, and wait for the officers to arrive."

That was it?

"What about Cam?" Aubrey's question was squeaky, but loud enough that the dispatcher heard it.

"Don't move the body, please." He was gentler with us now. "Help is on the way."

There weren't any sirens in the distance. Aubrey accepted Rory's offer of outstretched arms, and they staggered toward the house together. I should have been taking care of Aubrey, but she hadn't even looked at me again after I'd spoken to the emergency operator.

"You cut your feet," Liam whispered at my ear.

I shrugged. In the scheme of things, a couple nicks on my soles was nothing compared to what could have happened.

Liam slipped an arm around my lower back and another behind my knees, and then I was in his arms. I wrapped mine around his neck and tried to appreciate the easy strength with which he held me and the warmth of his chest. I tried to ignore the splatters of red marking our path to the house. The rain was already beginning to dilute the gory sight, thankfully.

I nuzzled closer until only the smell of the sea and his soap swirled around me. If I closed my eyes, I could almost pretend I was safe. I could pretend Liam would handle whatever came next.

It wouldn't be that simple, though. We weren't safe, not even in our perfect prom house.

# five

LIGHTS AND music roared to life farther up the path. The circuit breaker must have been flipped back on. Liam's steady pace faltered, and his arms tightened around me.

Noah called out from the pool, a teasing lilt in his voice. "What the eff happened to you?"

The green glow of the pool lights turned the red smudges on our arms and feet ghastly. It was the ghoulish green-gray of death. And it was all over the four of us.

Liam lowered me back to the ground gently before answering Noah. "It's Cam, man."

I leaned against the gate to the pool, feeling drained down to my very bones. The music pulsing beneath my palm no longer synced with the erratic beat of my heart. Water splashed my bare leg as Hudson cannonballed into the pool. Vic crashed in right after him, bobbing back above the water with his curly hair plastered to his forehead. The guys' laughter was loudest, but Dani and Holli joined in.

Cam was dead, and it didn't make sense. Why him? Why now? Someone should be screaming or crying or having some kind of emotional meltdown. Only none of us were. Aubrey was perched on a metal chair on the patio, her knees pulled tight to her chest. Her chest didn't heave with sobs, but her eyes were still ringed red.

Rory clung to her phone at Aub's side, typing without looking at the screen.

"What about Cam?" Noah asked, distracted.

Liam's hand held steady at my lower back. Was he the same guy who had leaped from the roof earlier? His jaw was locked tight enough I could see a muscle twitching in his temple. I should be weeping. Or calling my mom. She was going to lose her mind when she heard about this. She'd trusted me to leave for a weekend. Trusted me with Aubrey. Trusted me before college. Pretty sure being at a party where someone was murdered was going to make her rethink her trust in me. Hell, the idea of moving into the city for art school already made my head swim . . . and now *this*.

But I wasn't going to call her yet. Not until after the cops came. My skin was too tight and too hot, but my brain didn't care. Getting to safety came before everything else. Although, were we even safe from one another? There was no reason to think any of my friends would have hurt Cam, but my lizard brain said now wasn't the time to trust anyone.

My fingers twitched for a paintbrush or a pen, a way to sketch a path out of this. Having a goal was better than standing on the pool deck wearing someone else's blood and wondering how it could have happened.

Noah shifted from one foot to the other and peered around my shoulder. "Cam? Where is he?"

"D-d-down there." I inclined my head back toward the beach.

He started forward, but Liam held a shaky hand up. "Don't."

Noah stilled. Several strands of hair had escaped his loose bun. The salty air shook them like serpents. His lips thinned.

"Is everything . . . ," he started, his voice faltering.

The playlist shifted tracks, and a sob—Aubrey's or Rory's, I wasn't sure—slipped into the silence between songs. Hudson had pulled himself out of the pool. The corded muscles beneath his dark skin were still flexed. Water plinked onto the pool deck from his orange board shorts. The water was clear, but the dark spots it left below made me turn away.

A muscle in Noah's jaw ticked. This time his words were harder. "What happened?"

Hudson stood at Noah's side now. When had they all grown so much? All three towered inches above me, shadowed by both hints of beards and the house's eaves. Cam would have been the tallest, but he wasn't here. I sucked in a breath and tried not to shudder.

Liam told them what we knew. When he said it aloud, it didn't sound real. It was like the kind of ghost story Liam's eleven-year-old brother would tell. I suddenly heard it as it must have sounded to the dispatcher's ears and wasn't surprised he'd been so ready to dismiss us. The cops couldn't get here soon enough.

Hudson charged forward. "He might still be alive. Did you do CPR? Why didn't you bring him up here?"

Liam's hand disappeared from my waist and gripped the lacrosse player's broad shoulders. "He's not, and we don't know who did that to him."

Hudson didn't fight him, even though he could have won.

"We need to stay together," Noah said.

I swallowed against my panic. "The police said to go inside. We need to wait for them."

Hudson rolled his eyes. "We can't just leave him out there."

Noah stepped forward again, chest puffed like he was about to start something, but then his voice softened. "Staying close is the only way we make it through this."

Liam's brows pulled tight. "It's going to be fine, man."

"I'm calling my dad," Hudson said, already turning to get his phone.

Rory pushed her way into the tight circle of tall dudes. Her hair had begun to dry, sticking out erratically. I could relate. "Do you know if there's a first-aid kit or something?" she asked.

First aid was smart—we needed to clean the cuts on our feet—but . . . "We need to get everyone inside first." It came out harsher than I'd intended.

"You don't need to snap at me," she said. "You weren't the only one who saw that."

I wrapped my arms around my body, like they could hold me together. "I know. I'm just freaked."

"She's right," Liam said. The heat of his words brushed my cheek. "You two get Aubrey inside. We'll get everyone else."

"Holli's coming in with us," Rory said quickly. She glanced toward her girlfriend. The short Black girl had already pulled herself from the pool and was now kneeling next to Aubrey. "She called her mom, but the signal was garbage. So I guess we just need to wait for the police."

"Okay. We can figure out what to do after the cops come." Never had I thought I'd want the police to crash our party.

I followed Holli and Rory inside. Rory ushered Aubrey toward the bathroom. Hudson shoulder-checked me as he blustered through the house toward the front door.

"Hey!" I cupped a hand to my sore side.

His fist practically doubled in size as he squeezed his car keys. "I'm not waiting here for whatever comes next."

"You're bailing on Cam?" Incredulity curled my tone.

Noah ran through the living room to catch up with Hudson, Dani on his heels. "You can't just leave," I said as Noah brushed past me.

Hudson didn't even turn back. "Watch me."

Dani slowed her pursuit and hovered at my side. Had the testosterone in the room rooted her to the ground, too?

She coiled her long, dark hair around her fingers and then tossed it over her shoulder. "The cops are coming, Huddy. It isn't safe out there."

Hudson's fingers flexed against the keys. "I'm not interested in talking to the cops, babe, and I'm *really* not interested in hanging around when there's a murderer on the loose."

It made sense, but there was a gelatinous fear shaking in my gut that said we wouldn't be safer out there either.

Noah sidled between Hudson and the door. Mere inches separated his face from Hudson's. Noah had the height, but Hudson's broad chest swallowed Noah's form.

"The police said we should stay inside." Noah's voice was melodic, soft, and obviously trying.

Noah hadn't been on that call. I had. "It's true. The guy from nine-one-one told us to stay inside the house. You don't know who is out there. You can't have them follow your car. That's dangerous, too."

Hudson ignored me and looked down toward his chest, where Noah had rested his palm. "Get your hand off me."

"Sorry. Just trying to talk some sense into you," Noah said. "Leaving the house isn't the answer."

"Staying at the Shore with a killer sounds like a shit plan. I can get in my car and be home in under an hour." Hudson elbowed Noah away from the door, and then turned back toward us. "Dani, are you coming?"

Tears fell down Dani's cheeks. She didn't wipe them away. "You want me to lose you, too?"

Hudson's shoulders slumped and his chin dipped. "No, I—"

"Then stay," Dani rallied. "Stay here and help keep us safe."

Hudson slipped the keys back into his pocket and came closer to hug his girlfriend. "Yeah, fine. But after this, we leave."

I had been in Girl Scouts for a total of two and a half years in elementary school. Luckily, enough of those first-aid skills had stuck, and bandaging Aubrey's feet with a half dozen little butterfly adhesive strips had gone smoothly. She didn't whimper when we'd doused her soles with hydrogen peroxide. The red swirl down the drain had triggered my upchuck reflex, but I swallowed back the sickness.

Now wasn't about me. It couldn't be. Aubrey's lips were pale and flat. Her skin was cold. I still couldn't believe we hadn't even noticed Cam was gone earlier that night. What kind of friends did that? He slipped away at parties all the time. Telling myself that didn't make this easier. Didn't make my friend's hollow stare any less chilling.

"I think you're done." My feet ached, but I'd avoided getting any glass splinters. The lone cut next to my big toe had been easy to bandage. I went to the sink and rinsed soap from my hands. The water was clear with the white, sudsy foam. I blinked until I no longer imagined the pink streaks of blood that had been on my hands.

"Kylie." Holli's turquoise nails shimmered where she held my shoulder. Her brown eyes softened when I met her gaze. She'd transferred to our school this year and became part of our circle when she started dating Rory in February. She had delicate features set on a slender runner's frame and her brown skin was warm. Where Rory was brash and sharp edges, Holli was her punk rock kitten counterpart.

"Hmm?" was the best I could manage. My fingertips had gone numb beneath the cold tap water. My chest ached. I needed to call my mom.

"Rory is going to take Aubrey upstairs. You good?" She gave my shoulder a little squeeze.

I didn't bother lying. "Definitely not."

She huffed a non-laugh. "Same."

Holli headed upstairs. I snatched my phone off the charging pad and followed her. What else was I supposed to do? Stand here in the ground-level bathroom where I'd washed blood from my best friend's feet? Where I'd plucked pieces of glass from her skin? Maybe glass from the same broken bottle that had been used to murder her boyfriend? I wanted to bail on this house and this night. But I couldn't bail on Aubrey. I couldn't leave my friends to deal with the police and the aftermath. This was our last weekend before graduation. If I couldn't stick with them through this, keep everyone together and safe, then what would the summer hold?

I thumbed the phone screen to life. There were two missed calls and four messages from my mom. All were about the tropical storm simmering offshore and her regrets about letting me come to the beach. *If she only knew.* The need to call her and let her fix this rose in my throat, but this hadn't been some accident. Calling my mom would only bring her here, into the path of a killer.

There was a scream from Aubrey's room when I hit the landing. I went cold.

"Give it to me." Aubrey's screech penetrated the white, wooden door.

I bolted forward and slammed the door open into the room. It knocked into Rory's back and threw her forward. An orange pill bottle flipped onto the tufted cream rug and spilled its contents.

The slender yellow pills sprinkled the floor. Rory swore and dove for them. Aubrey was faster. My frozen friend from earlier practically snarled as she scooped up three of the pills. "What's the big deal?"

"What is happening here? Are you okay?" None of us were okay, but what was this?

"I just want to sleep. Chill out." I hadn't heard Aubrey that defensive since the time I'd called her out for listening to the new Taylor Swift album forty times in one weekend.

I turned from one friend to another. Rory ushered the rest of the spilled medicine back into its bottle, and Holli helped her from the floor. Aubrey had scuttled onto the bed, pressing herself back against the headboard. The white lattice of adhesive strips on the soles of her feet stared back at me.

"You didn't need to steal my Ativan," Rory muttered.

"You weren't going to give them to me." Aubrey stiffened like she was going to barrel toward her again. The headboard groaned.

I rushed to her side, sinking into the downy comforter. "The police will be here soon."

I'd meant it to be comforting. The fact someone else might handle this was appealing to me, but Aubrey recoiled. "I don't want to talk to them. I still have to call Cam's parents. Tell them he's . . . This night just needs to be over."

"We'll get through this." I didn't have the answers, but I hoped she could hear how much I wanted to help. I nodded down at the pills still clutched in Aubrey's hand. "Are you going to take those?"

"Rory took one." Aubrey's tone was petulant, but I ignored it. She pushed the trio of chill-out pills around on her palm.

"Yeah, because they're prescribed for me." Rory shoved her free hand through her black locks.

"She only took *one*," Holli offered, but wouldn't look directly at Aubrey. "It's probably fine for you to take one. My mom takes them when she flies, but popping a handful will make this night even worse."

I touched the tips of my fingers to Aubrey's wrist. Not stopping her, not grabbing, just touching. Her green eyes were bright, like grass after a storm, and rimmed red from crying.

Her chin dipped, only for a moment, but I'd known her long enough to recognize the agreement flickering in her gaze.

I edged more fully onto the bed, shuffling until my back was against the carved wooden headboard, too. It bit at my back, and I leaned into its bony pinch. This wasn't a dream or a nightmare; at least what was happening in this room was real. Aubrey was okay. Rory and Holli were, too. Maybe that would be enough for me to be okay, too? The cops would handle the worst of the night for us. They would find whoever had stabbed our friend, and we could go home, knowing we were safe.

Aubrey took a lone Ativan, and then slumped down onto the bed. Holli confiscated the remaining pills. "We're in the room below this one."

I nodded.

Aubrey curled into a ball beneath a bright blue throw blanket. Her toes poked out from the edges. She tucked the blanket to her chin and rested her head in my lap. I pulled the last few pins from her hair.

"It's going to be all right," I promised, like I had control over everything. I wasn't her fairy godmother, but I was her best friend and that required more effort anyway.

"Can it be?"

"It has to be." For me. For her. For Cam.

"I'd told him that if he was going to get shitty drunk he shouldn't have bothered to come." Her voice dipped to a delicate whisper.

The words might not have been meant for me, but I still answered. "This isn't your fault."

"You know what he said?" Her harsh laugh was a punch to my gut. "He said I was trying to stop him from having fun. Like it was about friendship. But *your* boyfriend didn't pour an

entire bottle of booze down his throat. He didn't get so drunk
that he . . ."

"Liam jumped off the roof tonight. Guys make dumb decisions. They aren't our fault and they don't mean they deserve
to . . ." I paused, unable to invoke death in this room. I settled
on "He didn't deserve that, and it isn't your fault."

Aubrey made a noncommittal sound. She snuggled into the
blanket and my lap a little deeper.

Music still stretched up the walls from the outdoor speakers. I couldn't make out the sound, but the wall's faint rattle
echoed in the headboard. Aubrey's breaths gradually slowed
and relaxed. A ridiculous part of me was jealous. She was
snoozing and I was alone with my disastrous thoughts.

What had drawn someone to this house? Was it the soli-
tude? The other Shore rentals were squeezed close, but ours
had breathing room. Noah had said it'd keep us from getting
noise complaints. My ribs squeezed tighter. We should have cut
the playlist. What if we were basically telling the person who
had stabbed Cam that we were still here?

Aubrey's shoulder blade dug into my thigh. I hissed, but she
didn't stir.

There was a soft rap on the door. When I looked up, Liam
stood in the doorway. Well, leaned. His shoulder kissed the
frame with a casual confidence. He hadn't bothered putting on
a shirt, and his golden skin gleamed.

I still wore a bikini, but at least I had a sleeping friend over
my lap. My stomach tightened.

His gaze flicked toward Aubrey. "She out?"

I nodded, and he took it as an invitation to come in. He
hesitated at the foot of the bed, as if realizing that we were

both less than half dressed. "Is the Wi-Fi down for you?" That wasn't the question he'd planned to ask.

I glanced toward Aubrey's nightstand and saw the LTE icon on my phone's screen. "Apparently."

He tucked his phone into one of the pockets in his shorts. "Wi-Fi's the least of our problems, I guess."

He wasn't wrong, but how did you reply to that? How did you respond when your new boyfriend was standing in front of you looking like pure candy, with that delicate softness in his gaze that he never wore around anyone else? How did you deal with seeing him here, just like you'd hoped, but only after discovering a dead body, after calling the police, after trauma?

The silence stretched from polite to awkward. He scrubbed a hand over his jaw. The inside of his palm was mottled magenta.

"What happened?" I asked automatically, my back easing away from the biting wood. His brows drew tight. "To your hand," I clarified. "Did you get cut?"

He clenched his fist. "It's nothing."

"Did you clean it out?" After seeing Aubrey's feet, tending hands would be nothing.

"Scrapes aren't a big deal," he responded half-heartedly.

I edged out from beneath Aubrey, slipped a pillow beneath her head, and tucked the blanket around her.

"There's a bathroom in the hall. Let me take a look."

I slipped out of the room on sore feet, and Liam followed.

# six

THE BATHROOM had seemed bigger when Aubrey and I were doing our hair for prom. The lighting had been bright enough I'd done my makeup sitting on the edge of the claw-foot tub while Aubrey hovered over the vanity, and my eyeliner had been fierce when we'd finished. But when Liam walked into the room with me, the space narrowed. My throat squeezed in response.

Our footsteps were swallowed by the oversized, plush pink mat at the center of the room. The slim pedestal sink bumped against my back, stilling me. When had Liam gotten so tall? So broad?

"What now?" The words scraped his throat. His bare chest was practically flexing with quickened breath.

Heat scrabbled up the sides of my neck. I tried to steal some of the remaining air, but he was simply too much in this room. He'd filled it, and now neither of us could breathe.

I dug my front teeth into my lip and hoped he didn't notice.

"Let me get a cloth," I said like it wasn't an excuse to look at anything other than him.

The door on the cabinet had the same weathered look as the shutters framing the windows, only slimmed down to half size. Inside was a small stack of washcloths, pale yellow and baby-shower green and first-day-of-spring pink. You didn't wash blood off with pastels, but those were my only options. I pulled the darkest cloth from the pack—powder blue—and started back toward the sink. At this rate we'd have to douse this house with bleach before we left.

"You don't have to do this." He was close enough that his breath skimmed my back.

"It's no big deal."

"Then why are you shaking?"

"I don't like small spaces." Not that I normally told anyone that. Maybe he wasn't just anyone.

It was one thing to kiss in the basement den at his house, but it was another to be fully alone together, sharing more than just simple touches. There was something personal, intimate about tending to wounds.

I squeezed my hands on the tiny towel until I was certain they wouldn't shake, and then I turned back to Liam. His right heel bounced against the floor. The rug blocked the sound, but the fluttering flex of his leg was unmistakable. Was he nervous to be here with me, too? Was it wrong to want him to be nervous?

"You should sit." I nodded toward the closed lid of the toilet.

"I'm good." The roughened tone suggested otherwise.

My laugh was too fast and short, like it'd been punched from my chest. "You've got blood on your hand."

Liam reeled back, eyes wide.

I quickly amended, "I didn't mean . . . I need to clean your hands. It's easier if you're closer to me."

Liam sat without further comment.

I turned on the tap and let the cool water rush over the cloth and my hands, welcoming the chill.

The bulbs above the vanity no longer carried the brilliant white of movie star setups that they seemed to have before prom; now they had the low smolder of a quality sepia filter. My eye makeup was smudged, but in this light everything was softer.

The firm line of Liam's jaw no longer pulsed, his chin no longer jutted proudly. His features were gentler in this light. His green eyes glowed beneath a fringe of dark lashes. The vulnerability stole my breath.

I stepped in front of him, holding an open palm beneath the damp cloth. My knees brushed his. A flash of awareness rippled over my skin until every thin hair on my forearm stood tall.

Liam pursed his lips but didn't say anything. His hands bounced in his lap, that right knee keeping time with music I couldn't hear.

"I need . . ." My voice faltered. *Get it together, Kylie. It's not like you're going to wash anything more than his hands.*

I cleared my throat, and Liam's gaze flicked to mine. It was heated and apprehensive, likely mirroring my own.

I tried again. "I need you to give me your hand." The words were soft, but solid.

One side of his mouth quirked up. "Oh, that would probably help. Sorry."

Staring at his lips was not going to improve the condition of his battered hands. My mouth went dry anyway.

He placed one of his hands atop mine. His hand was tanned and calloused and hot. "I've got this," I said to one of us, though I wasn't sure which one.

I dabbed the cloth against his skin and waited for him to hiss. He didn't whine, though, and I began to clean the wound. Dark flecks of red clung to the thin cotton loops of the wash-cloth. His fingertips had been caked in blood, but beneath it, the flesh was mottled. Purple and red marks speckled the pads of his fingers.

I pressed the cloth more firmly against his skin. "Does this hurt?"

He shrugged and gave an equally noncommittal grunt.

I cleared away the smudges of rust at the center of his hand. This time he flinched. I paused. "There's hydrogen peroxide downstairs. Want me to get that?"

"No, it's not that bad." That's what he kept saying, but I leaned closer. Two cuts ran parallel across his palm, one slicing right along the life line that Aubrey had spent all of eighth grade telling people she could "read." The cuts weren't clean, the skin ragged along the edges. If he'd accidentally placed his hand on the broken glass by the firepit, it should have punctured him. These were not puncture wounds.

How had Liam cut himself? I pulled the cloth over it again and ignored his sharp inhale. Blood welled again at my touch.

"These are worse than I thought." The truth bubbled from my lips. I tried to cover what was probably a *WTF* expression on my face with "We might need the peroxide."

"Nah. You can slap a bandage on it, and I'll be good." His hand was heavier in mine now.

"There isn't any glass in it." The fact sounded like an accusation. Maybe it was.

His other hand grazed my thigh. I startled and edged forward, my right leg now wedged between both of his.

"Kylie." He said my name reverently. And again, like a prayer: "Kylie, please look at me."

It was probably the lighting or the delicate way his mouth cradled my name, but I lifted my gaze to meet his. Those green eyes flickered like freshly cut emeralds.

"What happened?" It was my turn to plead.

*Make it good, make it true, make it not involve Cam or the broken glass plunged into the side of his neck.* It wasn't like a random bruise on your knee. You remembered a slash like that.

"It's just a cut." His gaze was direct, but that didn't make the answer any less of a dodge.

"I can see that. How did you get this?" I bit back my bigger question, not wanting to accuse him of anything when his bare legs against mine were warming more than my skin.

His eyes flared wide and then narrowed, like he could hear the real question. Like I'd actually asked him if he'd wielded a broken bottle as a weapon. He gulped hard enough that the ever-shrinking room amplified the sound.

My heart stuttered and my brain dialed up the adrenaline until even my toes quaked.

It took him three tries, but finally his raspy voice escaped. "The roof."

"What?"

Liam stood abruptly, before I had a chance to step back, and his chest pressed up against mine. I could feel his heartbeat tapping against my body.

I started to step backward, but his uninjured hand cupped my hip. "Don't."

"Liam—"

"It's not what you think. Fuck. I can't believe you'd think that, but it's been a night and I get that it's a lot and I don't know what's going on, but, Kylie, this"—there he was using my name again and holding his sliced palm above my shoulder—"is from climbing out on the roof."

I stopped trying to pull away. "How?"

"We kind of slipped out of that window, and I skidded down the shingles. It was probably a nail, but it isn't that deep."

A nail. The roof. That made a whole lot more sense than my boyfriend going all horror-movie mode on his friend. "You could have just said that."

His sheepish grin was ten times more powerful up close. "Burned up some skin like road rash, too, but better than falling off. That doesn't impress pretty girls."

The unease in my belly morphed into something more, something powerful and heady. I dropped the cloth onto the floor. *Splat.*

I pressed my damp palm against his chest, fingertips curled over the hard curve of his shoulder. "How many girls are you trying to impress?"

Liam tugged me into him, as if there were a way for us to be closer. He didn't hear the self-conscious truth buried in the question. Good. His hand disappeared from my hip and quickly found my chin. The touch was gentle, but commanding me to meet his gaze.

"Only the one that matters."

His mouth closed over mine.

I could taste electricity on my tongue when his lips skimmed mine, and it shot outward, singing from every nerve ending. Every place we touched simmered with potential, and there was so much of him. I slipped my hand around the nape of his neck. It was my turn to bring him closer.

The scent of mint and hops surrounded me. His groan rattled against my thumb. His fingers danced along my cheek, as if he were memorizing my features to replay them again later. He touched me like I was delicate, but kissed me with a fire that said I was unbreakable.

I pulled away, creating only the slightest whisper of space between us, and rasped, "Oh."

Liam's lips skimmed the outer edge of my ear. It was too soft to be a kiss, but I couldn't help my shudder of delight. His palm was broad at the center of my back as I arched into him. A finger slid beneath the tie of my bikini top, and the fire in my belly liquefied. My brain, however, short-circuited and I dug my fingers into his shoulders.

His husky laugh was a private sound only for me. "I've got you."

Got me how? I tried to turn my gaze toward him, but he held my chin more firmly.

"The only thing I wanted this weekend was to get to hold you like this." His breath was hot against my ear, but it was the *need* in his voice that skated down my spine and bit at something deeper, lower.

"The only thing?" My voice wasn't my own. It was velvet and honey. It was *sultry.*

That dark laugh again. This time his mouth was on my neck, searing this perfect moment into reality with each soft, wet kiss against my neck and shoulder.

A thunderous rumble erupted from the hallway. Hudson bounded from the stairwell toward us, whacking his fist against the banister every couple steps.

"What are you two doing?" Hudson had put on a shirt, but it was the panicked look he wore that sobered me.

I let go of Liam and tried to focus on the tingle in my fingertips, not the tension seeping back into my stomach.

"What does it look like we're doing, jackass?" Liam snapped.

"Ignoring the cops?" Hudson said.

I pushed away from Liam. The damp washcloth squelched under my heel. "The police . . ."

"Where are they?" Liam finished for me.

Suddenly I needed space, or I was going to puke. Our friend's dead body was still cooling on the sand, and I'd been so wrapped up in Liam that I'd forgotten. His kiss had made me forget a *murder.* What did that say about me? About us?

"Downstairs." Hudson folded one arm over his chest and gripped his bicep. It didn't hide how unnerved he was, but at least he was trying to stay calm. "They want to talk to you."

"Me?" Liam asked incredulously, like he hadn't been the one to call the cops.

Hudson rolled his eyes. "Everyone, but yeah, they want you guys to lead them down to Cam."

How nice of him to say *everyone*. Like Aubrey and I hadn't been the ones to find him. Like his blood hadn't been on Aubrey. Like Liam and Rory hadn't crashed into a crime scene, too.

The cops wanted to talk to everyone.

Why didn't that give me any comfort?

# seven

OFFICERS WOOD and Cooper didn't offer much consolation when we arrived downstairs. The latter corralled Liam, Rory, and me in the kitchen and asked us to walk him down to "the body." He actually said that. He made Cam a corpse. At least Aubrey wasn't down here to hear him. The others had told them she'd been there when we found Cam, and Holli had led Officer Wood upstairs to talk to her. Or try.

We led Officer Cooper out of the house and past the pool, toward Cam. The fairy lights over the deck had short-circuited in the rain. I ignored the chilly downpour and led the group across the dark expanse, Liam and Rory trudging behind. At least someone had remembered to stash the alcohol by the pool, I thought, and then felt a bubble of hysterical laughter threaten to burst out of me—the cops probably wouldn't care as much about the underaged drinking as they would the murder. I mentally shook myself; I needed to keep it together.

When we got to the gate, I gripped the rail but couldn't push it open. I gave it a rattling shake, but it didn't move. Liam laid his hand atop mine and then thumbed the gate latch up to release. The door swung open.

Officer Cooper didn't call me out, but I could feel that weird itch of his stare digging between my shoulder blades. Cop gaze burrowed deeper than teacher stare.

We crunched our way back to the firepit. Now Rory walked at my side, her hand clasping mine. Liam stayed close at my back. Gravel gave way to sand, and the storm raging in my belly iced over. I didn't want to see this again. I *couldn't*.

The police officer's flashlight beam bumped its way along the path, catching the shaggy edges of shells littering the ground and the teal paint on Rory's toes. None of us spoke. The thumping bass of the music was gone. Our voices were, too. This night had stolen them. Now we were left with Officer Cooper's not-so-subtle irritation. The narrowed eyes, the flat lips, the kind of repeated heavy sighs that suggested a severe breathing problem. He might as well have told us, *Your nightmare is my Friday night inconvenience.*

"He's just down here," I found myself saying.

Officer Cooper only lifted his chin in acknowledgment.

The sky was more than spitting specks of water at us. The flecks of rain plinked against the officer's radio. My mom's text messages flashed in my mind. The tropical storm raging over the ocean must have been stretching its fingers toward us. As if some rain could put more of a damper on our horrifying night. Salt permeated the air, and I pretended I could feel each granule against my skin. Pretended it skimmed my cheeks and added texture to my hair.

But with each soggy step forward, I knew something was

wrong. I could feel it in my gut, in the subtle, dark shifts in the electric night air. We approached the firepit.

Cam's body wasn't there.

Liam circled the firepit like a lone lap would change things. "He was *right* here."

"I knew it," the cop muttered. Then, louder, he continued, "Do you know how much of my time is wasted by your practical jokes? Another person in this city could actually be in danger, and I'm not there for them because I've spent my entire night responding to drunken teenagers who think it's funny to make up some tragedy on prom night."

I couldn't believe what I was—or rather *wasn't*—seeing. I scanned the saturated sand for the truth. My stomach twisted into even tighter knots, and I felt like I was on the verge of being sick. *Was* this an elaborate prank? Had someone slipped something in my drink? No, Rory, Liam, and Aubrey had been there, too. We'd all seen him, seen the body.

I didn't make this up.

"He was right here," I cried, but Officer Cooper didn't want to hear it. His hand wrapped around my upper arm, fingers digging in.

"This kind of prank is unacceptable," he snarled at me.

"Let her go," Liam snapped, his voice filled with malice. He lifted his phone and angled the camera at us. "I've got no problem live-streaming this."

The cop grumbled but released my arm. "There isn't anything to live-stream," he said. "All three of you need to get back in the house. I want IDs. You can't make claims like this without consequence."

Claims? There was a killer on the Jersey Shore right now. There might be one in the house now for all I knew. Someone had *murdered* Cam. I didn't know where his body had gone, but that only proved the threat was real.

"Maybe they took him," I blurted. "The killer. What if they're trying to cover it up?"

"C'mon." Officer Cooper nudged us toward the house.

I dug my heels in. "You can't believe we'd actually make this up. You can see his blood." I paused, realizing the rain had turned the sand into muddled dark spots. The proof had to still be there, right? "And what about all this broken glass?" Since when did I become bold enough to stand up to a cop? Oh, right, when there was a murderer on the loose.

"Let's go back in the house and discuss this." Did they teach that tone of calm-but-firm authority in the police academy? Officer Cooper shot me a dark look that even the bright, white beam from his Maglite couldn't obscure.

Maybe it was his poorly masked irritation with us, or the way his upper lip twitched like he was fighting his natural sneer at my pain. Or maybe it was that I'd called the police because we needed real help, and instead Officer Cooper stifled a yawn while I gaped at the scene where I'd found a friend dead.

"You aren't even going to look around, are you?" I said, my throat clenched.

"Miss." The honorific sounded like the equivalent of "little girl."

I waited. Rory's fingers tightened on my hand. "She's right," Rory said. "Your job is to investigate crimes. So *investigate*." I shot her a quick, grateful glance. She'd sucked in both lips, her mouth disappearing, but her dark eyes glittered with a dare for the cop.

Liam stepped toward me, phone still at the ready. Officer Cooper stretched out a hand, blocking Liam's path. My boyfriend arched a brow at the officer.

I wasn't the one to talk back to teachers. I hated sliding into a movie after they'd already dimmed the lights. I was a protest-through-artwork kind of woman. Ordering around an official member of the police department was not in my skill set, but I could still picture Cam's blood on Aubrey's hands. I could still see the blood pooling on his chest. I could still remember the iron tang on the air beneath the ocean spray.

"Our friend is dead."

"There's no—"

I didn't let him finish. "His body is gone. Either he wasn't really dead, and there is an injured teenager roaming the Jersey Shore right now, or someone took his body. Both of those options should matter to you."

"There's no evidence a crime even occurred." The cop leveled his stern gaze on us.

"If he's not dead, then you better be ready to explain why you didn't try to find an injured kid on your beach. His dad runs a real successful construction company, too. The nighttime news your boss watches will want to talk about that." Liam lifted his chin.

Rory dropped my hand, opting to plant it on her hip. "We shouldn't have to invoke bloggers or the news to get you to do your job."

"Our friend was murdered. Do something," I demanded with what was left of my crumbling courage.

# eight

OFFICER COOPER'S version of doing something was
walking us back to the house with the promise that he and Officer Wood would go back out and check out the firepit. They
weren't gone even five minutes before they'd returned to the
house from their so-called investigation. How much evidence
could they have gathered in five minutes?

Back in the living room, Officer Wood took pictures of
our IDs and told us Cam was pranking us and we shouldn't
take ourselves so seriously. Rory leaped to her feet, her fists
clenched, but Holli wrapped her arms around her girlfriend to
keep her from charging at the cops.

"Stay inside," Officer Wood warned.

"Because there's a killer outside?" Rory snapped.

"That storm turned inland. Call your parents and let them
know you're going to have to ride this out here. There's no way
you should be out in these conditions." He sounded exhausted.
Must be nice to be able to brush us off and still fake like he cared.

The police left, and the ten of us were on our own again. *Nine,*
I corrected myself. There were nine of us now. The math of

subtracting a human was too abstract and painful for my brain. We'd convened in the living room, piled on plush couches and stretched atop a rug that had once been flaxen and ruby before a sea of weekend renters had passed over it.

Hudson's arm stretched across the back of a dark blue love seat. Dani pulled a foot up onto the cushion and hooked her hand around her knee. Her legs were long and toned from cross-country season. Hudson's fingers teased at her shoulder, but she shrugged off his touch.

Liam lingered at the edge of the room. The eyes that had glimmered for me upstairs were now staring at the front door. Maybe he was waiting for the police to return with apologies. A flare of envy shot to my jaw, and I clenched my teeth. Tonight's dismissal had hit me harder than it had him. He still had hope someone else would find Cam, would help him, would help us. I didn't know why, but I knew better.

"How does a guy named Wood ever get laid?" Vic was a year younger than us. Noah had invited him to the prom house to fill one extra bed. He wore the kind of perpetual sneer that would have made him the cute, mischievous kid in junior high but that just looked obnoxious now. He had stretched his compact frame out on the rug in front of the couch. As his bare feet clapped an unfamiliar beat against the metal legs of the coffee table, it was clear he didn't feel out of place. Even if half of us had grumbled at his invite.

Holli snapped her fingers next to his ear, his fidgeting clearly riding her nerves. He barely twitched.

"C'mon. Uniform might do it for some people, but he might as well have pinned 'Officer Hard-On' to his chest." Vic doubled down in a way that made only Noah laugh.

It wasn't just that the joke wasn't funny, it was the timing. We'd lost a friend—figuratively and literally—and the people who were supposed to do something about it had just bailed on us. And all this guy could think to say was some weak dick joke? Pass.

Vic pressed up from the floor and rested his forearms on the glass top of the table. Despite being the shortest person in the room, he seemed to be taking up a significant amount of space, especially for a guy we barely knew.

Why Noah was determined to befriend this kid was beyond me. He'd had good taste in friends before. How did the potential of being a fifth-year senior make him befriend this guy? Why he'd invite him to be his stag buddy for prom or stay at this house? Noah hadn't spent time with anyone outside of our class until this semester. Vic wasn't even in any of my classes and he had only been to three or four of Liam's "required watching" movie nights, but now he was a part of our circle.

"What now?" Vic asked, like it was time for keg stands instead of bolting the doors to keep out a killer.

The room rumbled as thunder shook the wooden eaves of the house. Holli bolted upright at the sound. Her wide eyes turned to the bay window behind us. Lightning flashed outside, followed quickly by another skyward shudder. Dani jerked her shoulder away from Hudson. Her fingernails pressed into her shins hard enough I could see the impressions from a few feet away.

I shook my head. We were all trying to find the right thing to say. "I'm going to see if Aubrey will come down here. We aren't talking about next steps without her."

"Isn't she sleeping?" Noah's genuine concern cut through my rising frustration.

My arms were wrapped across my stomach, the light squeeze of a self-hug was almost automatic. My words were softer this time. "Probably, but we shouldn't leave her alone right now."

I started toward the stairs.

Liam's brows practically knitted together, consternation written all over his face. At least his attention was back on me, even if it was no longer lit with desire. "You want me to come with?" Liam whispered in my ear, the worry in his voice apparent.

I declined with a quick shake of my head. I could climb stairs on my own. Freaked or not, there was no reason I couldn't go upstairs by myself. This wasn't a horror movie where going deeper in the house had bloody consequences. I stalled on the first landing as that thought flitted through my mind. *Bloody? Really, brain?* I gripped the railing, fingers turning white. They were clean. No red marred them, but anxiety flared in my tummy regardless. Stomach acid wasn't logical, it seemed.

We needed a plan. Procedures worked for me. It was like sitting down at the pottery wheel. It was relaxing when I did it right, but if I didn't have enough water on my fingers, if I didn't prepare the clay properly, if I ignored metering my foot on the pedal, everything splattered, and I had to start over.

That's what this was. I needed to collect my friends, needed to get us to regroup, needed to have a plan to get answers about Cam and to keep the rest of us safe from whoever had done *that* to him.

Step one was getting Aubrey. I released the handrail and started climbing the steps again. My palm prickled, blood rushing back into it with a heated rush.

Waking Aubrey was always a dangerous endeavor—many a sleepover had taught me that lesson—but I hoped the anti-anxiety medicine still coursing through her veins would keep me from getting smacked with a flopping arm.

That hope was unnecessary, though.

Aubrey was already awake.

And she was shrieking.

# nine

I BOLTED up the final steps, Liam thundering my name from a flight below. I wasn't going to wait on him. I banged open the door to her room and blasted inside. The queen-sized bed was empty, blanket bunched at the base. Her dull pink weekender bag slouched in a cream club chair in the far corner. The navy-and-gold shimmer of her discarded prom dress was pooled at its feet.

Aubrey was at the other end of the room, standing at the open window. She must have seen me. Her strangled keening became a choked cry. I was at her side in four long steps. Her waterproof mascara had held, but her eyes were still ringed in red.

I scanned the room again, confirming we were truly alone. No bogeymen, no murderer. Just the two of us in a farmhouse-chic rented room.

Liam burst into the room, winded and searching the space for a threat. "Kylie?" His throat squeezed my name.

I held up a hand, and he stilled near the doorway. "I'm fine. It was Aubrey, and I don't know what's wrong yet."

I turned to my friend. "Aub, are you hurt?"

It was a dumb question. Her features screwed into a *Seriously?* look, and I deserved it.

More footsteps rang out from the hallway. Liam nodded in my direction and stepped out of the room. I heard him whispering to the others, but I couldn't make out the words. Whatever he said kept anyone from barging inside.

I wrapped Aubrey in my arms without thinking, but she elbowed me away. The brush-off hurt more than her elbow to my ribs. Both of her hands clung to her phone, her thumb urgently tapping the same spot again and again.

"It's gone." The screen held her full attention. She tapped it again.

I craned my neck to see her phone. She was trying to open the photo albums.

"What's gone?" I asked, concern leaking into the question.

"It won't let me see him." Aubrey sounded like she was on the verge of another meltdown. I made my voice as calm as possible.

"What do you mean? See who?"

"Cam. All our videos, every private video message. They're not here. I need to see him." She tapped the icon for videos again. An alert popped on the screen. *No Internet.* She dismissed it, tried to open the album again, and the cycle repeated.

My mouth went dry. I tried to swallow anyway. We'd already lost a friend, walked over broken glass, and been disregarded by the cops. Would saying the wrong thing make everything worse?

Screw it. "Did you join the Wi-Fi? I think the password is 'eatabanana' all lowercase."

Holli had announced the password earlier in the afternoon and Rory had immediately said she wasn't about to let a Wi-Fi password tell her how to live her life. Hudson had pointed out they hadn't provided bananas for us, and so they couldn't be that concerned with our potassium intake. Trying to remember the banana jokes didn't do anything for the wrecking ball of anxiety trying to collapse my chest.

"I'm on the Wi-Fi," she snapped.

I checked my phone. I had another four missed calls from Mom and two from Dad, which were probably Mom. Her texts had gone from "be careful about the storm" to "you need to come home" to "CALL ME!" I checked for bars, but the signal had gone out, probably from the storm.

"Well, maybe—" I scrambled for some perfect answer.

"Not 'maybe' anything. I tried turning off the Wi-Fi. There's no 5G, no crappy 3G, no data at all. There's no connection, and I'm a dumbass who put all my videos and pics of me and Cam in the cloud because Dad said I didn't need the storage of a bigger phone. The only one saved on my actual phone is the lock screen."

She locked the phone and turned it toward me.

It was a picture from spring break. Cam was wearing Aubrey's electric-green sunglasses. She was on his lap. Neither looked at the camera, both wholly fixated on each other. Their smiles were huge enough you could hear the laughter in the still image.

"We can get Vic or Noah to reset the router." They'd taken programming class electives. Hard pass for me, but maybe they'd also be able to figure out why we went from four bars of service a couple hours ago to no-man's-land.

61

She muttered an agreement, but returned to tapping her screen.

"Aubrey," I coaxed. "I want you to come downstairs with me."

"They don't need me there to reset the router."

No, but I needed her there. I needed her to be part of this. I needed to keep her safe.

"The police came by while you were resting . . ."

Aubrey pursed her lips. "I know."

I said her name again, and she cut her eyes toward me. "We need to make some decisions about what to do now, and you should be there."

Her jaw hardened.

A spike of irritation skated my chest, easing the weight digging into it and sobering me. "I don't want you to be alone."

When she opened her mouth to argue again, I cut her off. "Everyone heard your scream. They're in the hallway. So either you come downstairs or they're going to come in here, but we're safer together."

The caramel flecks in her eyes warmed, and she nodded.

She believed me. Now I just had to hope I wasn't wrong.

Both Vic and Noah took runs at the router and proclaimed it functioning. Other than the whole no-Internet part.

"The box works fine. Not a hardware problem." Vic had his laptop open atop his folded legs. He was back on the carpet.

Noah whipped his long, dirty-blond hair up into a loose bun. He'd dropped onto a floor spot next to Vic. "Must be an outage from the storm." The knot in my chest tightened as he confirmed my suspicions.

All nine of us had gathered in the living room, but so far all we'd discovered was that none of us had any cellular connection. Both Vic and I had tried calling our parents, but the lines were truly down. My mom overreacted a lot, but knowing she wasn't an option only made me want to pull my friends closer.

Holli and Rory had been huddled on one end of the long couch, but they'd pulled Aubrey between them once she came down. I'd planned to stay close, but my best friend had clasped her free hand with Holli's and that was okay, too.

"A Wi-Fi and data outage? At the same time?" Hudson had a tablet in his palm and stared at it like he could will the Wi-Fi into action. It'd be a formidable superpower, but it hadn't manifested yet. Dani's feet were braced against his thigh, her back against the other end of the love seat. She swiped from screen to screen on her phone with the same amount of luck as her boyfriend.

"Could that storm really jack with it?" Dani asked.

The sprinkling patter earlier had shifted to heavy sheets of rain. The sky had darkened beyond the bay window in the living room, but the steady *whoosh*ing of wave after wave of water dropping from above wasn't subtle.

"I'd check the hurricane tracker, but . . ." Rory had already put her phone away.

I'd slipped on a pair of denim cutoffs and wedged my phone in the back pocket.

"If cell data crashed every time it rained, we'd still be living in the nineties." The snark in Liam's voice took me aback. He waved me over to the extra-wide chair he'd commandeered next to the unlit fireplace.

I slipped in next to him, our hips pressed firmly together. His arm dropped around my shoulders. The added weight behind my neck was surprisingly comforting. My heartbeat eased to a relaxed rhythm, and I leaned into his side.

Hudson drank from a long-necked beer, then placed it back on the coffee table. The heavy clank of the bottle meeting the glass made Aubrey jump. I edged forward to go to her, but Holli squeezed her hand and whispered in her ear. Right. It was covered. We were a team. All of us. Together in this.

"You guys are making this too hard," Hudson said, maybe to all of us, maybe just to Vic and Noah. He popped up from the couch, jostling his girlfriend. "If signal sucks in here, we go out there."

Noah shot up from the floor, but Dani was faster. She gripped Hudson's wrist. "It's bad out there, babe. And the cops said to stay in."

"The cops also said that we made up a murder." Hudson's carelessness cut across my chest.

Liam squeezed me closer, but no one moved.

Shocked silence had a thickness to it, I realized. It clogged your pores and filled your throat. Aubrey broke the quiet not with a cry, but with a question. "Did the police use their phones while they were here?"

No one replied for a long moment.

"Officer Cooper definitely didn't. We weren't with the other one the whole time." My throat ached as I forced a note of calm into my voice. I swallowed, and Liam pressed a quick kiss to my temple.

"He used the radio clipped to his shoulder. That was all I saw," he added.

"Wood"—Vic snickered—"didn't use a phone either."

"So let's pop out onto the porch and see if there's a signal," Hudson said like we were all idiots.

That got Rory out of her seat. She blocked the path to the front door and took a long gulp from her beer bottle. "You're not going out there."

"You going to stop me?" His laugh was of the asshole tough-guy variety.

He'd clearly never met Rory for coffee after her Saturday morning jiujitsu. I'd watched her jam her shoulder into a big guy's hip and throw him to the ground hard enough that he didn't get up for a solid minute.

"I shouldn't have to," she replied.

"She's right," Holli chimed in. "It's not safe."

Hudson scoffed. "Of course you agree with her. You're sleeping with her."

Liam stood at that, and I found my feet right behind him.

"Dude, not cool." Liam held up a placating hand. "This storm is getting bad, and we don't know who is out there. It's not like we've got city streetlights here. We won't be able to see who is watching us."

I scrunched my toes against the hardwood. There were three large windows opposite Liam and me that looked to the street and were only covered with gauzy white fabric. The rain beat against the glass, flying toward us practically sideways. Could the person who killed Cam be standing out there now? If he could kill one person, wicked weather wasn't going to stop him from killing more. Was he watching us and getting off on our terror? Was he planning another attack? I edged backward until the chair's textured fabric pressed against my calves.

Holli's cheeks had lost their rosy hue. Aubrey tucked the tip of her thumb in her mouth. I wasn't the only one putting it together.

Rory's exasperated huff kicked across the room. "The cops might have dismissed us, but you know full well what happened out there."

Hudson folded his arms across his chest, his tablet tapping against his hip. "I didn't see it."

# ten

THE SPRINKLING of rain that had speckled my shoulders and spritzed my face earlier was now a legit downpour. Water droplets whizzed past the open railing of the porch with sharp, cutting strokes, pelting the concrete and asphalt of the yard. The water was already collecting into a soggy marsh over the small grassy plot.

I lingered at the doorway, not ready to step out onto the wooden slats of the porch. Liam was pressed to my back, his chin above my shoulder.

"Hud, man, you're not going to get service in this." Liam's plea sounded sensible.

At least to me. Hudson? Not so much. He held his phone aloft, like raising it toward the slanted roof could call forth the cell phone reception gods. He edged toward the front of the porch. Smudged glass covered the lone bulb in the front porch light. Its rays strained against the glowering storm to illuminate a path.

Dani shoved past me out onto the porch. "Get your ass inside," she yelled at Hudson.

"Waiting around in this house is a dumb move." Hudson was right. Unfortunately, when your options were limited, you had to go with the least dumb move.

Dani grabbed his wrist. "It's flooding, and it isn't about to get better when it's beating down like this."

Lightning cracked the sky and struck one of the utility poles at the street. The box at the top began to spark.

Dani let out a cry and threw one hand in front of her, as if shielding herself from the yellow-gold sparks falling from the singed tower. I had jumped at the crack of lightning; now, with my pulse skittering, I yelled, "Come on, guys. *Please.*"

A thick muscle ticked in Hudson's jaw. He stared at his girlfriend like he'd never seen her before.

Noah stepped past me, edging to the railing. There was a wariness in his hazel eyes I wasn't familiar with. He kept a solid six feet between himself and Hudson.

His voice made up for the distance, even over the roar of the rain. "Kylie's right. Come back inside. Leaving your girlfriend alone is a bad move."

A dark flame lit in Noah's pupils. The sky was still shimmering with a steady stream of sparks from the shot electrical box on the far tower.

Hudson stalked toward Noah. "You're one to talk about bad moves."

Dani squeezed Hudson's arm but only said, "Babe."

He stilled.

The ocean was still hidden in shadows, but the squalls screamed. The waves beat the shore with abandon, and each powerful crash shook me like the threat of bone-on-bone. This wasn't my first big storm. I'd weathered hurricanes before. We lived farther inland, but we'd still had the flooding. My dad would crank the generator and my mom wouldn't call me out if I broke into the hurricane snacks too early. This was a tropical storm. It shouldn't be shaking the house. It shouldn't be shaking *me*.

*Shouldn't* didn't mean a lot when the boards beneath your feet were beginning to flutter.

"This storm is going to get worse," Hudson announced, as if we all hadn't been telling him that exact thing.

"Let's get back inside before it does." Dani's black hair whipped around her head as a gust of frigid, salty air scoured us.

Hudson tugged her toward the steps. "Or we could get in the car and get out of here before every road is flooded and we're stuck in this house for days."

Without warning, the front yard lit like a flash grenade. I shut my eyes on instinct, but the white halos had embossed themselves onto my eyelids.

Back inside.

We needed to be in the house, and we needed to be there now.

# eleven

HOT WHITE and orange streaks shot from the tips of the downed twin power lines, their rubber bodies bowing and coiling in the water from where they'd snapped and fallen into the flooded front yard. The bright flashes of light had lessened after that initial burst, but the hissing of electricity that charged the liquid surrounding the live wires was a constant whisper beneath the sputtering rumble of the incoming tropical storm. Sparks from the utility pole floated down to the water-covered yard. Flash flooding was an understatement. Our lawn was now a deadly electrical accident just waiting to happen—and Hudson seemed determined to walk right into it.

"Hudson, no!" Dani yelped. She'd wrapped her hands around his wrist as he moved away from her.

Her boyfriend shook her grip off and stumbled toward the stairs. Liam darted past me, and he and Noah grabbed him by the shoulders, catching him before he could stumble away from the wraparound porch's protection.

Hudson thrashed between his friends' holds, a riot of expletives exploding from deep in his chest in a string of snarls.

"You don't get to make decisions for me," Hudson snapped.

"We do if you're going to get yourself killed." I could hear the effort it took to hold his friend in Liam's weary voice.

Hudson rolled a shoulder down and punched it back, catching Liam hard in the chest. His grip slipped, and Hudson snatched his newly free hand up to pull free of Noah's fingers. "I can handle the storm."

Silhouetted by the bright sparks of the felled power lines, Dani balled her fists and punched at Hudson's biceps. "You idiot!" she yelled. "Stop it, before you get hurt!"

*Enough,* I thought. These were my friends. I'd come to this house with the goal of testing the waters with Liam, to get a taste of actual freedom. If I had to keep everyone from killing themselves and each other to get there, then I guessed I was stuck being the sane one.

Some of the bramble had blown onto the porch in the midst of the storm. A branch the length of my forearm teetered on the nearby chair. I grabbed it.

"Guys?"

They ignored me. Liam and Noah struggled to get a new hold on Hudson's arm, their bare feet grappling for purchase on the wet wood. The lacrosse player started forward again, Dani still screaming after him.

"You can't go out there," I yelled. The storm tried to steal my voice, but I wasn't here to barter away my chances. We needed to get back inside, we needed to regroup, and we needed to find a way to make it out of this place without any additional tragedies.

I stepped toward the railing. The sky spat its warning at me. Icy flecks of water assaulted my cheeks. The windows to my right were dark, but I could feel the eyes of the rest of the group watching from inside. Good. They needed to see this, too.

I threw the branch out in front of the steps, directly where Hudson was trying to charge. Electricity shot through the branch, bright and burning, before the water could douse the flames.

"The hell?" Hudson said.

"How'd you know how to do that?" Liam asked at the same time Dani questioned, "I thought you were shit at science?"

"I was into electroplating for a minute," I said so softly I doubted they truly heard me. Now wasn't the time to talk about the science of electricity in water. It was time to get inside.

"That"—I pointed past the steps, to the fallen power lines still charged with power, and beyond that, to the dark wall of the incoming wallop of what my mom had called Tropical Storm Winston—"can kill you. We've already lost one friend tonight. I'm not losing another."

"She's right. Tonight we need to stay close." Noah's somber words were loud enough to push back the storm.

The tension choking the air around us softened. Liam's arm grazed my lower back, his hand slipping around to cup my hip.

"Thank you," he whispered against my ear.

I nodded, unable to give him more. Hudson could have died. I could have seen a second dead body in a single day. There was no help coming tonight. If we couldn't get out of here, no one could come in. The police wouldn't be back. They wouldn't be seeking Cam's body. They wouldn't be hunting a killer.

It was that fact, and not Liam's fingertips tapping against

my hip bone, that cooled my skin and commanded every fine hair on my body to rise.

We were well and truly alone.

Dani stormed into the house first, swearing and nearly in tears. Slowly the rest of the group paraded through the door. The storm was swelling, water slipping sideways onto the porch. My shirt clung to my back like a sopping rag, and yet I held at the rail. Sparks shimmered from the corner of my eye.

Liam's heel bounced against the aging porch planks. If not for the harrowing roar of the rain, I would have heard it creaking beneath him. "You coming in?"

I nodded and followed him back to the living room. We latched the door behind us, but it groaned against the growing wind.

The interior of the house had gone completely dark. *Power outage.* It wasn't the normal nighttime darkness that came with tendrils of starlight and the filtered moon. That had all been blotted out by our unwanted guest Winston, who had likely upgraded from a tropical storm to a hurricane by now. Liam swiped open his phone and tapped on the flashlight. I squinted against the thin beam of light. It cast a narrow path to the living room, and I stepped forward carefully.

Rory tilted her lit-up screen skyward, but both she and Holli had their gazes trained on Noah. He, too, had his phone illuminated, and steered Hudson around the coffee table to the farthest seat from the door. I couldn't have been the only one who noticed that, but Hud didn't complain. He dropped onto the short couch where Dani was cradling her shin.

No one sat on the floor this time. I opened my own phone. The battery was already at 76 percent. Oh well, the flashlight couldn't suck up too much energy, right? Rory and Holli continued to hold vigil around Aubrey, the only person in the room who didn't look like they were contemplating puking all over the furniture.

I couldn't follow Liam back to the chair. I couldn't sit again. Static snapped against my legs. Standing still wasn't an option either. Vic stalked behind Dani and Hudson, a short stocky shadow bobbing back and forth, halfway blocked by the love seat. At least I wasn't the only one unable to sit down.

"I've got a camping lantern in my bag. Back in a sec," Noah announced. He trotted off up the stairs.

"Did he say camping lantern?" Dani asked.

I was close enough to see the hint of Liam's shrug. "Dude brings everything everywhere."

I scrubbed a hand over my eyes. It didn't make the world brighter, but it bought me a moment.

"There were candles in the pantry by that nasty bottle of gin," I said. Finding them would give me something to do.

Aubrey was still sandwiched between Holli and Rory, who were having some kind of intense conversation using only eyebrows. I wasn't about to get in the middle of whatever that was, but I couldn't stop looking at Aubrey. Her upper teeth worried at her lower lip, and even in the awkward glow from the phone flashlight I couldn't have missed her wan features.

"Aub?" I said her name just loud enough for her to hear, lest everyone hear how desperate I was for her to react.

Her eyelashes fluttered. "Hmm?" Her voice was so soft I might have imagined it.

"I'm going to find some candles. Do you want to come with me?" Doing something had to be better than going catatonic on the couch. It had to help her cope, right?

Her brow furrowed, but before she could say anything, Rory said, "We've got her."

My eyebrows jumped up at that. "I just thought she'd—"

Rory leaned forward, knocking over the empty beer bottle she'd left on the floor. "She's set."

Heat flared in my cheeks. I cast one last look at Aubrey, but when she didn't raise her gaze, I turned on my heel and left the room, the sting of Rory's admonishment chasing after me.

# twelve

MY BEDROOM—at least, my temporary digs—looked different by the time I'd climbed the three flights and flung open the door into the dark. It somehow seemed smaller now; the climbing vines on the wallpaper that had once looked lush now seemed sinister.

Liam placed a lit pillar candle and his upturned phone on the nightstand, flashlight on, the natural and artificial lights warring. I could see more of the room, but now I was just imagining snipers hiding behind the green trellis on the walls. I ran my nails down the side of my neck. Maybe this was a bad idea.

We needed more light, more people, more air.

"Are you sure we should leave Aubrey with Noah and Vic?" I closed the worn white door to my bedroom in the rented house, even as I fought a phantom urge to crack it open again.

My best friend hadn't wanted me. I told myself it was because I'd been there when we'd found Cam, but it didn't make it hurt any less. So Noah and Vic had volunteered to camp out on the floor in Aubrey's bedroom across the hall.

"They'll watch out for her." Liam dropped onto the end of the bed, and his confidence didn't waver.

Could I siphon some of that? I arched a brow. "We are talking about Vic . . ."

"Vic and *Noah*." He invoked his best friend's name like Noah was the lead of a SWAT team, not the lanky dude who had brought a hand-crank radio to prom party weekend.

Concern flickered beneath my breastbone. "I'm not seeing him as the caretaker type. Aubrey is . . . delicate."

It was his turn to cock a brow. I'd forgotten he'd once seen her argue that tardy points shouldn't affect her grades because they didn't have anything to do with her final work product. She'd done it in front of an entire classroom after—you guessed it—showing up late to class, and while she'd earned a sly smile from our history teacher, he'd still docked the points.

"Okay. So. *Usually* she'd be able to handle them, but in this state? Her boyfriend just died. She's not normal now."

What was wrong with me that I'd just leave Aubrey like that? My best friend had lost her boyfriend, and here I was across the hall with some guy. My emotions were shot, but so were hers. Could I pretend this was self-preservation and not just me wanting alone time with Liam? Shame slicked my insides. She needed me, and I wasn't about to punk out on her now. I shouldn't leave her with friends she didn't know as well as she knew me.

I turned back to the door. Liam cleared his throat, but that didn't stop my gripping the bronze knob.

"None of us are normal right now." Pain choked his words. That rasp of honesty ricocheted between my ribs, plinking against the worry that had been woven there. I released the doorknob and met his eyes.

He rested his elbows atop his knees, a hunched pregame prep pose that looked different—*haunted*—in the dark. I couldn't say he was going to cry, but wetness glistened at the corners of each eye. Liam was broken, too, and while his lips didn't move, it didn't change the question he was asking: *Will you help me?*

Damn it. How had my weekend gone from cute bikinis and pretty dresses to tears and death? Why didn't I want to say no to him? I rested a hand on his shoulder. It quivered beneath my touch. I sat down next to him.

"You really think Noah will be able to help Aubrey?" I leaned my shoulder against his.

"She's probably already asleep," he said, but then quickly added, "but either way, Noah is probably the best person to be with tonight."

I couldn't quite smile yet, but I let a little worry ease from my tone. "Is that so?"

"I'm not saying *you* should be with him." Liam propped his hands behind him and leaned back. His torso stretched beside me. How tall was he again? "I'm just saying Noah is the Boy Scout. He knows every emergency move. He thought to bring a lantern. I just brought board shorts."

"You really weren't ever in Boy Scouts?"

His emerald eyes dimmed. I didn't know why that hurt him, but I hated that I added another shadow to this night with a single question.

"No, I wanted to be." Distance crept between us, but Liam kept going. "Noah was already a Cub Scout when we became friends. I asked and asked and asked my dad to let me join. He finally did."

"I thought—" I started to ask.

"It was just a few months. Doesn't count."

I bit my bottom lip to keep from saying more. I was bad at small talk, bad at romantic talk, and apparently not doing so hot on the whole consoling talk.

Liam sucked in a big breath, the sound rasping against his teeth. His chest expanded, his shirt edging up enough to let the tops of his hip bones peek at me. I stared. I shouldn't have. Not right now. But I did.

"My dad wouldn't show up to help me with any of the stuff I needed to do for patches. So I had to quit. No point in being in Scouts if you don't do any of the Scout stuff, you know?"

My heart ached for him. I forgot about his exposed skin and met his gaze again. The corner of his mouth quirked up. He'd caught me staring, and it'd gone straight to his head. Well, that's one way to cheer someone up.

"What does your dad do?"

"Sales." He said the word like it could stamp a period on the end of any conversation.

I didn't get sales as a job. Not that I couldn't comprehend the idea of selling goods or services, but that anyone would want their life's work summed up in one, overly vague term. There had to be more, right?

"What does he sell?"

"Financial software to accountants. Lots of flying all over for trade shows or meetings or who knows. He's gone twenty-five days of every month and has been since I was a kid."

"That sucks." Understatement.

Liam shrugged. "I'm used to it."

He wasn't lying, but that almost made it worse. "It was a miracle that my mom didn't follow me to the Shore house and stake it out on the beach," I said at last.

He cast a sidelong glance toward the window, and then pressed a kiss to the cap of my shoulder. "Are you sure she didn't?"

I could almost picture it: Mom with a black bandana over her hair and matching oversized sunglasses covering half her face. My mother was a lot of things, but sneaky was not one of them. "She would have knocked down the door when she saw a cop car."

"Or when there was a tropical storm warning?" There was more warmth to him now.

"That too." I eased back to mirror Liam's position, and hoped he couldn't see the doofy grin that was making my face ache. The plush duvet didn't offer much stability. I pressed my side firmly against his for balance.

"My mom . . ." Should I tell him more? He'd told me about his family, but mine was *complicated.* "Things weren't great— or safe—when I was little."

"Your mom bakes cookies, Kylie."

I got it. Reconciling my mom's always-around, always-hovering, always-giving ways with anything less than watch-ful was hard to imagine. Sometimes I even forgot what it had been like with my bio dad in the picture. "She does, and it's good now."

"But it wasn't?" he prompts.

I licked my lips to buy time. "My biological dad wasn't

great. Mom and him together were worse. Like full-on tsunami bad."

Liam nodded slowly. Was he processing this information or realigning me into some pity column? I didn't tell people about my bio dad, and this was why.

"My stepdad is basically my dad, and he's great. No big deal. My mom is still compensating for when it wasn't great. That's all." I was babbling. Great.

Liam shrugged. "I get it."

"You do?"

He nodded, and silence tugged between us.

"What do you think is happening out there?" His heart beat against my ribs, and I didn't have to turn to know he wasn't looking out at the rain pelting the window.

Now it was my turn to shrug, and it highlighted just how close we were. It didn't matter that we now had more clothing on than we had before, when I was cleaning up his wound. We were on a bed. Alone. The realization chimed like the middle C on a piano inside my chest. Could he feel that, too?

I was supposed to be thinking about my friends. I was supposed to be worrying over a killer. I blurted out the first thing I could think of to distract myself from the heat of him against me. "My mom is probably calling my phone now."

Liam chuckled. "If cell towers are down here, they're down everywhere."

I licked my lips, like it'd bring the right words forward, but it only reminded me of how soft his had been when we'd kissed earlier. I scrunched the duvet in my hands until the soft fabric was bunched in my fists.

"She'd worry." *Weak conversation, Kylie. Don't push back into downer territory. You're here with your boyfriend who wants to give you a moment of peace. Get it together.*

Liam tapped his ankle against mine. There was no heat in the move, no pressure. "I'm not too bad in an emergency, even without Noah's Boy Scout tricks. Growing up fending for yourself has its perks. You don't freak out when it starts storming and you're home alone."

"We're not alone," I corrected. Did I always sound so breathy?

"That makes it better."

It was cheesy, but heat licked the sides of my neck regardless.

"Really, though, I picked up enough when I was a kid that now I can handle myself. I *should* be able to handle this, but . . ." Liam shook his head, and that flop of dark hair fell forward, skimming his piercing eyes. "None of this has been right."

"What do you mean?"

In a single, smooth motion, Liam sat up and turned toward me, his palm cradling my jaw. Warmth flooded my chest, and I leaned into his touch. The bedroom wasn't too small now, it wasn't too dark. Not with him here.

"This." He kissed me delicately. It was light and dizzying and gone too soon, like swiped champagne on New Year's Eve. "That should have happened earlier."

We'd kissed before, but I couldn't correct him. We hadn't kissed like *that*. Not soft or slow or with a razor of panic threatening us. I lowered my gaze, but that only made it clear to me that Liam's shirt was straining across his broad chest. I remembered the honeyed skin beneath it. Was it still heated?

Would his muscles flex beneath my fingers? Liam's hand lingered on my face, and tiny bubbles of delight fluttered up from my abdomen. Would he tremble beneath my touch? I kept my hands firmly planted on the bed. This could escalate quickly. Did I want it to?

*Should* I want it to?

"I wanted to make this weekend special." Liam's thumb traced a tiny circle on my cheek. How could such a simple move make my heart race?

"Me too," I said automatically.

"I wanted to get you flowers." His eyes cut away for a half second, and all I could think was that there were never going to be flowers. But I wouldn't have cared before, and I definitely didn't care right now.

I pressed one hand to Liam's chest. My knuckles ached from gripping the comforter, but Liam's soft intake of breath made me forget any soreness. "Flowers are overrated."

He swallowed hard. "At least there are candles."

The small, white pillars flickered from the nightstand and dresser. The orange glow softened Liam's profile and lit a tiny flame in his eyes.

"I didn't think you could get more beautiful." There was awe to his words.

On any other night, it might not have been enough; I might have questioned his motives, my reactions. But after a night filled with unspeakable horror and fear, I didn't have any energy left to deny my own feelings.

I dug my fingers into the fabric of his shirt and then yanked him to me. His hard chest knocked into mine, and I tumbled backward onto the bed. He followed, heavy and solid atop me.

"I'm learning plans are for suckers. Tonight was horrible at every turn, except with you. So, if not for you, I'd be . . ." My voice cracked, and I couldn't finish.

Liam didn't need me to. He leaned down and covered my mouth with another slow, delicate kiss.

# thirteen

FOUR IN the morning was supposed to be one of those quiet hours. It was the time when parties usually broke up, crumbling into factions of wandering hopefuls and sleepy drunks. It was the time of night when I usually tiptoed back into my house and did the careful dodge of the squeaky floorboards to avoid waking my stepdad. Not that he was ever actually asleep, but we'd brokered a deal that if I didn't wake Mom, he'd pretend I'd come home at curfew.

It felt strange and more than a little bit spooky walking through this house at 4:00 a.m., where none of the noises were familiar to me. Wind howled against the house, whipping against the windows and rattling the glass. My bedroom door opened with a whine. I shot a glance back to a still-naked Liam, but he didn't stir. The bedside candle was almost burned out, but the tangerine and copper glow still softened his features. His dark hair was mussed from both my hands and the pillow. The sharp angles of his cheekbones were softened in sleep in a way that stirred a protective tightness behind my heart. Saliva moistened his lips, and after having them pressed up against me, I couldn't even be grossed out by that.

If everything else this weekend went to hell, at least I had this. I had *him.* My abdomen fluttered at the thought. I lifted my phone and its flashlight—and tried to ignore that the battery had dropped by 10 percent while I was snoozing in Liam's arms. *I'll turn it off when I get back upstairs.*

The hallway was eerie, though, and I didn't think it was just the rattling of the tropical storm against the windows or the groaning floorboards beneath my feet. I could only see a couple of feet in front of me, and that made the framed artwork on the walls lose its kitsch. I'd watched too many spooky movies, I told myself, but that didn't stop my skin from crawling like the shadows were stalking my every step.

I nudged open Aubrey's door, because despite her promises that she was fine and had no problem taking consolation from everyone else but me, I needed to see her for myself. Her arms were flopped over her head on the bed, her mouth parted in a soft and steady buzz of snoring. Vic had squished two throw pillows into a haphazard ball. He dozed atop them near the foot of the bed. Noah must have been around the other edge of the bed, but I didn't need to check on him. Aubrey was safe and asleep.

I shook off my worries and swallowed against the unease clinging to the roof of my mouth. I needed to hurry down three flights, snag a bottle of water from the cooler, and get my butt back in bed next to my boyfriend.

My bare feet clapped on the steps, despite my careful footing. Sand on the steps clung to my heel. The dull roar of the ocean and the offshore cyclone quieted as I reached the bottom of the first flight. I lifted my phone's flashlight and discovered there weren't any windows on this floor. Maybe in the bedrooms, but there was no way to peek at the shore or the pool from this vantage, even if the storm hadn't blotted the moon and stars from the sky. If Hudson and Dani hadn't commandeered a room on this floor before I'd even arrived, I would have tried to swap with Holli and Rory. Or bunk with Liam and Noah, who were supposed to be splitting a room on this floor. There *was* a spare bedroom here, now that I thought about it. Would it be safer for us to move down a flight in case the storm upped to a cat three?

A heavy *thunk* resounded to my right. I stilled. Who else was here? Who else was awake? The closest door—Dani and Hudson's room—remained shut. I sidled closer and pressed my ear to the door.

*You make one executive decision to save someone's life, and now you think you're ready to take care of everyone? Get yourself together, Kylie.*

I should have kept going. Water. Liam. Sleep. That was the plan, right? Only I caught Dani's harsh whisper through the door. It was that kind of stage whisper the drama kids used. All emphatic and not that quiet.

"It's not like that," she said.

"I've seen him in your room." Hudson's barb shot like a knife through the quiet night.

Any semblance of whispering was dashed. "We live together!"

Aging wood creaked from within the room. Were they moving closer to the door? Farther away? I wanted to see so badly but didn't dare move.

"I've seen Noah in your room before your dad got with his mom," Hudson retorted. I'd known Dani's dad and Noah's mom were dating, but not that it was serious. Not living-together serious.

Dani let out a long breath, loud enough to reach into the hallway. "Just drop it. I told you it's nothing."

"Seriously?" Hudson huffed. "Don't act like I'm the asshole here."

"Oh, so I'm an asshole for being friends with my step-brother?"

"You're not related." There was a hardness in Hudson's voice I hadn't heard before. It was sharper than his earlier determined pleas to get out of this house. A bedroom door couldn't muffle that kind of hollow desperation.

The door across from Dani's creaked. Rory or Holli? I pressed my phone against my chest to hide the flashlight, but no light peeked from the other doorway. The hallway air was thick and static. Was I the only one hearing this fight?

"No, but we've been friends for years." Dani didn't hide her exhaustion. "*You've* been friends with him. You can't expect me to ignore Noah."

"He wants you."

"So?"

"So? That's all you've got?" Their door shook with a single pound of a knock. Hudson's fist? 

I jerked back, but couldn't leave. I should have. This conversation wasn't for me. Hudson and Dani were notoriously on and off, but was he really suggesting she had anything going with Noah? I guess Noah was hot in a rangy nerd way, but he wasn't Dani's type.

"Either you trust me or you don't. I'm wearing your shirt right now, not his. I'm staying in a room with you, not him. I don't know what else you need, Hud, but this jealousy shit is getting old."

Dani never shared much about her and Hudson's conflicts with me. Mostly she wanted to regale the group with a highlight reel of their best antics. Had every breakup been over this? Over him thinking she was cheating? I wouldn't have put up with that, but then maybe that's why she hadn't told me. Paranoia was the opposite of sexy.

"He wants you. It's not subtle."

"I'm not doing this. *He*"—she tossed the pronoun like a gauntlet—"is sleeping in Aubrey's room and Liam's bunking with Kylie, so you can have this room to yourself. I'm taking the empty room—the one with zero jackasses—and getting some sleep. Try not to be such an asshole in the morning."

*Crap crap crap.* I spun and shot down the stairway without thinking. My heel slipped on the cool wood, and I flailed to grab the handrail. My shoulder cried at the twinge, but my grip stopped me from tumbling down at least another seven steps. My phone flipped out of my hand and clunked four times before skidding to a stop on the landing below.

The flashlight beam lit up the dark.

*Crap crap CRAP,* I thought again, holding my breath and trying to stay as quiet as possible.

Then a door slammed behind me, loud enough to make me jump. I lingered, holding on to the rail as if even a fractional movement would give me away.

I waited in the dark until my pulse slowed and my breathing evened out again, but no one came after me.

# fourteen

A TALL, skinny woman watched me from a picture frame mounted on the wall. My cell phone's light stretched upward to capture the woman's pin curls. In the glow of the flashlight, the frame looked almost inky, like the paint was fresh and not some 40-percent-off deal from the craft store. I had plenty of those frames. They were on sale the same alternating weeks as the acrylic paints.

The woman's sidelong glance was probably coy in the era of the photograph, but I swore she was watching me. "Please don't follow me," I muttered as I crept down the hall.

The stairs opened to the front foyer. My feet sank into the plush, round rug. I was quiet, but the hinges on the front door whined. Wind howled, snapping around the house. I didn't need Wi-Fi to surmise the storm was more than tropical at this point. The owner of this place should have given us plywood or secured the shutters just in case. He hadn't, though, and it wasn't like we could contact him now.

The white battery icon at the top of my phone lost another

line. *Right. Water. Liam. Sleep.* I scurried into the living room, the bay window offering no moonlight tonight.

Rain pummeled the glass, and the vast darkness of the storm beyond the panes was possibly more unnerving than the creepy photography lining the stairs. I could barely make out the railing on the front porch. The vibrant white wood wrapping around the house was now a shimmering streak only illuminated in momentary flashes of far-off lightning.

"You can't sleep either?"

I screamed at the voice. Legit screamed. If I'd been outside, the storm would have snatched the sound and squelched it. As it was, the rattling of the glass and the groaning wood of the house must have dampened the sound for everyone upstairs.

No one came running.

Was this how Cam had felt? Did the killer know no one would hear us scream now?

Noah lifted a campfire lantern close to his face. "Chill. It's me."

The small but powerful light distorted his features. It was funhouse lighting, but he was still Noah. Still Liam's best friend. Still the guy I'd left to watch over Aubrey.

I clapped a hand to my mouth and left it there long after sound pushed past my lips.

"You cool?" His tone suggested I did not look cool.

I nodded slowly and deliberately, because I was not actually okay. My heart was still beating hard enough I could swear my sternum was vibrating.

He lowered the lantern to his side, and it lit most of the room. I toggled off my phone's flashlight to conserve battery.

Boy Scout Noah had none of my nerves. "You're extra jumpy. It's just a noisy storm. No big."

"Our friend died tonight, and then his body disappeared. There's a killer out there somewhere." *Or in here?* The anger and fear building behind my breastbone rushed out of me in one big breath. He probably didn't deserve to be snapped at like this, but I couldn't let guilt lap at me when he was so being so blasé.

"We're inside, though," he said defensively.

I gaped at him, because what the actual eff?

The groove between his eyebrows smoothed in a flash. "I'm not saying I'm not freaked, too. But if nothing else, this storm is keeping us safe. As long as we're all together inside, we're good."

I wrapped my arms around my torso. Why hadn't I brought a long sweater? "Sure."

"I mean, we have an electrified moat." He laughed at his own joke.

I didn't, but I admitted, "There is that."

"Kitchen?" He hiked a thumb over his shoulder toward the adjacent room.

"What brought you down here?" I asked as we walked toward the kitchen. "I thought you were crashing with Vic and Aubrey." I swallowed. My throat still felt like sandpaper.

"Couldn't sleep," he said plainly.

The kitchen windows were smaller, but there were more of them. Each small square shook with the force of the gales. I stayed close to the center wall. If that glass shattered, I wasn't planning to get new wounds.

"Moat or not, today was a lot." He deflated with the admission. Shoulders slumping, fingers releasing the lantern onto the countertop.

"Understatement." I lifted the white lid of the nearest cooler and tugged a water bottle from the icy center. I held it aloft. "You want one?"

He shook his head and sauntered to the blue cooler next to the back door. The four panes of glass in the door were only covered by gauzy fabric. A blast of water rushed against the side of the house. The lamp cast enough light to show the water sloshing onto the patio out back.

"Get away from there." My voice shook with fear.

Noah plucked a beer bottle from the cooler, and then popped the cap against the counter with the heel of his hand. Spending the middle of the night in a ghastly kitchen with someone else who was drinking when I was in water mode wasn't appealing, but it had to be better than running into Dani on the way back to my room.

Noah took a hearty swig before saying, "I'm surprised Liam didn't come down with you."

That stopped me. "Why's that?"

He shrugged, but wouldn't meet my gaze. "He's really into you."

I ducked my head, hoping he wouldn't see the sparks of delight that had to be lighting up all over my face.

"You've known him a long time, right?" I knew the answer but asked anyway.

"Since before we had adult teeth." Noah laughed to himself. There was a story there, but it wasn't for me. He shook off the mirth. "You're special to him, you know?"

Liam had made me feel that way tonight, but everything still had that shimmering *new* quality to it. He was broad and firm and had a laugh that could shake this house when he let it free. But none of that guaranteed we were endgame. I wanted us to be.

I propped my hip against the counter. It was a casual move. Not at all about steadying myself. "You think?"

I focused on the icy bottle in my hand, the serrated edge of the cap between my index finger and thumb. The little prick of plastic was almost enough to distract me from how badly I wanted to hear what Liam had said about me.

"Obviously." Noah's sudden cough forced me to look at him. Really look. He worried his lower lip beneath his front teeth.

"I'm pretty into him, too," I said. It shouldn't have made me blush. I'd just been mostly naked in the same bed with the guy, but talking about him without him in the room offered a different kind of exposure.

"He checks his phone every three seconds for messages from you like he doesn't know how to turn on notifications. I was a little worried you might be making him dumber." There was sourness beneath his joke.

"In fairness, I do message him a lot." So much so that Aub or Rory would demand we go airplane mode for an hour, no messaging.

"It's cool." He leaned back to drink from his beer. The silence quickly got awkward. "You're cool. And good for him. Where you going to school again?"

My chest squeezed. I wasn't supposed to know about Noah being held back.

"NYU. They do a kind of cool interdisciplinary program for art studies." I stretched my fingers like I was pressing them into soft porcelain clay and not into 95-percent-recycled plastic.

Was I supposed to just play along here? I couldn't ask him where *he* was going to college.

"Right. He told me that," Noah muttered against the mouth of the beer bottle, and then took another sip. After he swallowed, he continued, "That'll work. He's going to Rutgers, you know."

I nodded, though my stomach sloshed. This night just got weirder by the second. Would Dani be settled in the other bed yet? A squall slapped the side of the house with a sickening splash. *Hard same, storm.*

Liam and I had talked about acceptance letters—he'd applied all over—but we also had kind of avoided talking logistics. New York and New Jersey were close. I went into the city all the time now. But being on the other side of the Hudson might change that. Would he come in to see me? Would I want him to? In the last few hours, we had settled on solid ground; now, imagining the memorization of train schedules and mapping logistics the fall might bring, I felt like I had been tipped off-kilter.

"I didn't think he was going to stay in Newark, but it's going to work out great." Noah wasn't looking at me anymore. He pulled another beer from the cooler, not noticing the snap and scrape of small branches and dark leaves slapping up against the window over the kitchen sink, or the whoosh of the water rushing them away. "He's probably going to live at home. He'll still be right next to me. Nothing has to change, really."

Was he serious? Right now it felt like everything was changing. I didn't ask about his plans. He didn't need me upping his anxiety, but how long was he going to try to keep this secret? "I didn't realize he was going to live at home that first year. NYU likes you to live in the dorms, but that's cool for you guys."

Noah startled, the corner of his top lip curling. He set the beer on the counter with a heavy clang. "Bet they won't let him crash in your dorm."

I caught my breath, and the counter bit into my back, cold and steady, as I leaned away from him. "One thing at a time," I said, not at all prepared to talk overnights with Liam with some other dude. Even if said dude was his best friend.

Noah scrambled forward, hands held high in supplication.

"Sorry sorry sorry," he said in a rush. "I'm all up in my head tonight. I thought I knew what this weekend was going to be like, and then Cam . . ."

I screwed the cap back onto my water before saying anything. It wasn't so much that I needed the time to recover as I thought he did. "None of us could have been prepared for that."

No one expects their friends to die. No one expects a murder.

Noah stared at me. Seconds stretched to minutes and his watery gaze pinched at my skin.

Finally, remorse dripping from his every pore, he said, "I should have been."

When he slammed back the entire bottle of beer, I couldn't judge him. Because I was just as guilty.

I'd lost track of the number of hurricanes I'd weathered. Or at least the number that had threatened New Jersey with imminent flooding and outages and then had resulted in ankle-deep flooding, uprooted trees, and an evening without electricity. Real storms? The kind that shattered windows and left you stranded without water and power for days on end? We'd only had one of those in my memory.

Tropical Storm Winston was supposed to be the former. Mom wouldn't have let me come to the Shore—upcoming birthday or not—if there had been even an inkling that this storm might have the oomph to track with a real category rating.

And yet it was a bellowing roar of a hurricane that woke me for the second time that awful night.

Liam's arm was heavy across my ribs. I pushed it aside, and his whole body shifted until he was flopped onto his back. His eyelids fluttered but didn't lift. It couldn't have been more than an hour since I'd come back to bed from my late-night water break, and my body ached from the fitful sleep I'd gotten.

Another roar rumbled, and then another. Each blast of thunder was shorter and louder than the last. I picked up the yellow plastic lighter from the desk and scraped my thumb across the metal wheel until a flame ignited. I lit a fresh pillar candle and then padded around the bed.

The closer I stepped to the window, the more clearly I could pick up the steady, wet whoosh of rain against the house.

There was another roar, this one distinctly human. The sound came from the floor below us, and it was dark and primal and definitely not the wind. My heart stuttered.

It only took a moment to shake Liam awake and another for him to dispel the fuzziness of sleep.

His brows pinched when his eyes finally cleared. "Kylie? Are you okay?"

His hands sought my arms, skimming over my skin like his fingers alone could find and repair any wound.

"I'm—" I didn't know how to answer, but I didn't have to.

Liam shot to his feet at the sound of another bellow from downstairs. "What the hell is that?"

We stepped out onto the landing, and I moved in front of Liam. Another version of me would have let him lead. Or, you know, stayed put in the safety of my bedroom. But that version hadn't washed blood from her friend's body. She hadn't been the voice of reason that kept everyone else alive. Those streaming documentary series I watched always had some crying lady telling you that everything changed in an instant. They were usually talking about snapping before killing their husbands. But there was something to that idea. The last twenty-four hours had changed me.

Aubrey's door opened, and Vic stumbled forward. "What is that sound?"

A masculine roar reached the landing, and I didn't wait to explain. I started down the stairs, Liam at my heels, both of us holding our phone flashlights aloft. The dreadful roars I'd mistaken for Winston's winds whipping the house transformed into deeper, nastier howls with every couple steps. The unintelligible shouting became discernable words by the time I stormed past the narrow woman's picture with her admonishing gaze, onto the second-floor landing.

"No," that masculine voice howled. There was a smacking sound, like a fist smashing through plaster. "No."

"Stop," another voice demanded.

"No." *Smack.* And it continued.

I rounded the final landing and stopped. Liam caught

himself before he sent me tumbling, but his arm shot around my waist with a protective pull.

"Kylie?" His voice shook, and I could feel more than see his attention fixed on my face.

What did I look like? Was I panicked? Had I gone green? I wanted to fixate on the paneled front door, the black sky beyond the inlaid glass. I tried to focus on the ornate rug, the one that had cushioned my feet hours ago. A small camp light rested on the floor at the base of the stairs, making it easy to see.

Easy to see the tears streaking Hudson's cheeks and the blood seeping from his knuckles as he bashed them into the nearest wall.

Easy to see the bruise growing bold beneath Noah's left eye.

Easy to see the black seeping into the thick pile.

Easy to see the pebbles of plaster sprinkled across the wood floor and sticking in the viscous liquid.

Easy to see the white bone popping from a mangled arm.

Easy to see a neck twisted too far to the left and tilted too far back.

Easy to see Dani's body broken at the bottom of the stairs.

# fifteen

I COULDN'T make myself go down there. Taking the next step meant putting myself back into this situation again. Another dead body. Another dead friend. Sickness sloshed up the back of my throat. I swallowed it down instead of adding to the mess.

Liam released me and hurried down the remaining steps. It was his turn to be the responsible one. He said Hudson's name a few times, but Hudson kept throwing punches at the wall.

"Noah?" he tried. Noah just shook his head and stared at Dani's lifeless face.

Liam placed a hand on Hudson's shoulder, and it stilled the next throw.

"What happened, man?" Liam asked Hudson with the pliant tone of a counselor.

Hudson swiped a hand over his Mohawk. "You tell me."

Just hours ago, his words had been all commands and confidence. Now there was a note of desperation in his voice. That got me moving down the stairs. I lingered on the last one.

Stepping down put me next to Dani's body. It put me near her blood. It put me in a crime scene. Again.

"Dani?" I said her name softly, as if she were a toddler I was babysitting and I didn't want to wake her from a nap.

Dani wasn't going to wake no matter how loud I spoke. The unnatural angle of her jaw was clearer up close. A raspberry bruise made a hatchwork pattern from beneath her ear to the tip of her chin. Her eyes were wide open, but the light behind them had disappeared.

"Who could have done this?" Hudson's voice broke on a sob.

"You . . . you weren't here?" Liam's poker face was garbage.

Hudson rounded on him. While Liam had height, Hudson had the bulk, and when he puffed his chest, it looked like Hudson could swallow the world. "The fuck? No."

My eyes stung, but I willed away the tears. Our friend was dead at my feet. I didn't have the emotional capacity to watch my boyfriend get pummeled, but the distraction helped me shove my feelings down. "Hud? When did you find her?"

His eyes widened and searched the room, manic, ready for a fight. A challenge rumbled from deep within his chest.

"He found her." Hudson glared at Noah, who still hadn't lifted his gaze.

"Noah?" I tried. "What happened?"

Noah ignored me, like he ignored everyone else in the room. His fingers twitched at his side, but his bare feet didn't move. He loomed there, unmoving.

Hudson deflated as quickly as he'd rallied. "I . . . I . . . I just came down the stairs and she was there."

Maybe Hudson had only needed someone to side with him. Only I wasn't certain I did.

"What do you mean?" Liam asked, the question so direct he might as well have poked Hudson in the chest.

"What do you think I mean?" Hudson's nostrils flared, and the *dumbass* at the end of his sentence was silent. "I mean I came downstairs to scrounge for food and found my girlfriend like this with that jackoff standing there all catatonic."

He extended his hand toward Dani's limp body. Drywall crusted his reddened knuckles. He snatched them back close to his chest a second later. Blood was soaking the carpet, but death was beginning to permeate the walls.

My stomach flipped, and I dug my molars into the side of my cheek until the pain demanded mental focus. Could Hudson have done this? I remembered his accusations behind that paneled door last night.

"When did she go downstairs?" I asked. Would he admit they had slept in separate rooms? Would he tell us they'd fought last night? Did he know I'd heard them?

"Don't know." His answer was fast. *Too fast?*

Dani's blood was seeping across the carpet toward me, but I couldn't move. Like Noah. What did *he* know?

Liam picked up the palm-sized camp light from the floor. There was a cracked divot in the wall near the stairs. Roughly a foot above the baseboard. It wasn't marred red like the hole from Hudson's punches a few feet higher.

"You wake up when I flush the toilet two doors down. How did you miss your girlfriend climbing out of bed?" Liam's tone was pure disbelief but devoid of accusation. He tilted his head to watch his friend, like maybe Hudson had hit his head, too.

Hudson's fingers twitched at his side, his index finger popping in front and then behind his ring finger over and over. "I didn't say I didn't know she'd gotten up. I don't know *when*. Turned my phone off to keep the battery. No clock."

The knot in my chest tightened.

I'd never thought of Hudson as clever. It didn't have a thing to do with his jock status; that was a ridiculous stereotype. It was the straight-line answer he picked for every problem. He always took the quickest path out. Like when he'd tried to bolt out on the group yesterday. Leaving Dani might have been more drama than it was worth for him.

"Did you go back to sleep?" I wanted to ask if Dani had eventually returned to his bed, but I wanted to keep the secret of their fight in my pocket.

"Why are you asking about what I was doing? What are we going to do about her?" Hudson's voice shot up an octave.

"You're right," Liam said, his face drawn and voice grave. "We need to figure out what to do."

"You give Noah that black eye?" The vitriol in Vic's voice startled me more than the reminder that he stood on the stairs. Holli was quaking in Rory's arms behind him.

Hudson simply rolled his eyes.

Vic took two steps down to be fully in the foyer. "You going to punch me, too?"

"I can't do this." Hudson's words were hollow.

"Come on." Liam started toward the living room, the camp light bobbing from its little metal handle and illuminating the blood and the bone and Hudson's balled hands. I picked at my nails but didn't move.

"We can't leave her." I had barely whispered, but both boys stopped.

I edged closer, keeping my toes two inches from the blood line, until I could kneel near Dani's head. I ignored Noah's cold stare. Twin locks of hair bisected Dani's face, their smooth curves cleaner than the jagged skin on her broken forearm. I swiped them back using only the very tips of my fingers. Tears tracked fiery paths down my face.

"You aren't supposed to touch—" Liam started.

My glare stopped him.

Small clumps of white plaster sat like melting snowflakes at the crown of her head. The dark liquid matting her hair and tacking the rubble in place was camouflaged in her black locks, at least in this light. If the sun broke through this storm, if it stretched in bright and golden from the window in the front door, the vibrant, violent red of blood would be undeniable. I didn't need to see it now to feel the horror of what had happened to her in my bones.

"Oh, Dani," I said close to her ear. She needed to hear the apology in it, even if she was gone. I shouldn't have fled down the stairs. Maybe if I'd brought her downstairs with me for a drink with Noah, she'd still be here. Maybe if I'd brought her back upstairs and let her crash with me and Liam, she wouldn't be lying broken and torn.

"The stairs are slick, but I don't get it," Hudson muttered.

I'd skidded on the stairs, too. They weren't crafted for bare feet at speed. But purple and blue ringed Dani's wrists, I noticed. She hadn't had those mottled bruises yesterday.

I swallowed hard. Liam edged closer to me and stretched

a hand out. "Come sit down. We'll be close enough to see her, and we can figure it out."

Figure it out? Liam was as new to this cool, collected, in-charge thing as I was, and it showed. Dani was dead. Cam was dead. We'd lost two friends in less than twelve hours. Slick stairs or not, Dani had been murdered, too.

And my gut said someone in this house knew something.

I lifted my gaze past Liam's open palm, past his wide, be-seeching eyes, to stare directly at Hudson. His jaw was locked tight, the muscle in his temple twitching. His arms were folded over his chest like some bouncer about to call me out on a fake ID.

Kneeling next to the girl with the snapped bones, broken neck, and oozing head wound, though, I wasn't scared of him.

Maybe I should have been.

I gathered every bit of grit I possessed and said, "This wasn't an accident. Someone killed Dani, too."

# sixteen

THE LIVING room had been leeched of color. The sun was probably up, but it couldn't penetrate the roiling storm clouds. Hurricanes had a way of plummeting the world into darkness.

It was 8:47 a.m. and my phone battery had dwindled to 39 percent. The NO SERVICE message was still displayed in pristine white text at the top of my phone, over the lock screen photo of me and Liam at a movie night just a few weeks before. I should have powered it down. Several of the others had, but one of us needed to keep it on in case a signal reappeared. It'd been wishful thinking before, but now, more than ever, we needed help. We needed to call the cops, and this time, they would have to listen to us.

I glanced to the right—to Dani—and the sigh that slipped past my lips was filled with defeat. Straightening my shoulders, I tried to will steel into my spine. I couldn't call anyone yet, but that didn't mean we had to let this stand. We didn't have to wait for another person to die before we took action. It's why I'd demanded everyone come together after Cam's death.

Doing something had to staunch the grief, right?

Noah had disappeared into the living room without a word after the confrontation, but I'd stood vigil over Dani's corpse while Liam had gathered a sheet from one of the upstairs beds. He and Vic draped it over her body. It hid the unnatural angles of her neck and arm and disguised the bruising and the blood beneath three-hundred-thread-count linen. The rug was still covered in her blood, though, and that darkness stretched beyond the edges of the sheet toward the living room, reaching for me, asking why I hadn't been able to intervene.

I refused to acknowledge the guilt pooling in my stomach or the tears clawing behind my eyes. Holli's soft sobs were muffled by her girlfriend's shoulder, but Rory scanned the room like she could spot the next threat in the shadows.

When Aubrey finally came down, she crumpled at the base of the stairs, and I half carried her to the couch. Her weight lolled to the right against the arm and away from Holli on the center cushion.

Now Hudson cradled a throw pillow against his chest. "Okay, we're all here. Are you happy?"

*Happy?* Hardly. "It's better that we are all together." It was the most truthful thing I could say.

"Better?" Hudson scoffed. He gripped the pillow like he intended to chuck it at me, but he resisted.

Aubrey's voice was lilting and quiet, but there was a current of strength in her words. "Being alone doesn't work."

I nodded to her, where she was now upright on the sofa. Her eyes were puffy and red, but her pupils were sharp.

"We're going to talk about what happened," I said like I already had the facts. "And if we're going to do that, we're doing it together."

"Who put you in charge?" Hudson's voice wasn't loud, but it didn't have to be.

I opened my mouth to say something—I wasn't sure what—but Rory beat me to it. "He's got a point."

*What?* I blinked hard enough that tears could have fallen. "I'm trying to help."

"You said the cops would help." Rory's words were slurred. Condensation clung to the outside of the brown bottle in her hand. Apparently beer with breakfast was a thing now . . . or at least it was when your friends were being picked off one by one.

"She also said staying here would make things better." The pillow seams were going to burst if Hudson twisted the fabric any tighter. "And now my girlfriend is dead."

My nerves were raw. "I found you and Noah with her body. Not sure how you think her death is my fault."

Hudson's eyes narrowed, but before he could tell me *exactly* how I was to blame, Liam intervened. "We heard the cops' advice. That wasn't Kylie, and if it weren't for her, you would have dunked yourself into electrified floodwater. So maybe back off."

Liam angled himself closer to me like a shield. Did he think Hudson would get violent? I hadn't considered it until I'd seen Noah's black eye. How well did I really know the people in this room? Was one of them truly capable of murder?

Hudson huffed but didn't say more.

"So the new plan is to talk about everything and try to piece together how this could have happened." Liam recapped everything but looked to me for confirmation.

I simply nodded.

Vic turned his back to the foyer, to Dani's body. He plopped an open container of orange juice on the coffee table. "Because our plans worked so great before?"

"Where'd you get that?" Holli asked, her red-rimmed eyes on the OJ.

"You're really asking about a goddamned beverage right now?" Noah scratched at his forearm and then his knee, hands fluttering with a chaos that made me uneasy. They were the first words he'd said since we'd found Dani's body.

Rory met his anger note for note. "If it was in a cooler that was labeled for Holli, then yeah, we are. She's diabetic, you asshole. She needs the sugar at the right time."

Vic pushed the container across the table toward Holli. His muffled "sorry" sounded genuine.

Rory gripped the edges of the couch cushions next to her knees. I recognized that move. She was digging in for a fight, and it wasn't really about Holli. It was about the broken body fifteen feet away. It was about losing another friend.

I almost felt bad about stealing the outlet from her, but I needed to do something useful.

"Someone killed Dani," I said bluntly.

Half the room looked to Hudson or Noah, the other half gaped at me. As if the dull blade behind my words hadn't cut me open, too.

Dani's boyfriend's cheeks turned ruddy. "I told you—"

Liam cut him off. "You told us you found her and Noah. We know." He sat next to Hudson on the love seat. He stretched a hand toward the lacrosse player's shoulder but didn't make contact. "Kylie wanted to bring everyone here so we could all hear it once. Save you from saying it over and over."

That was not why I had wanted everyone in this room, but

I didn't correct Liam. Hudson's anger ebbed enough for him to grind out, "I found her like that. Noah was just lurking over her like some psycho."

Noah glowered at our friend, anger rolling off him. The muscle in his jaw ticked, and it was more than the accusation. What did he know? Had he heard Hudson and Dani's fight, too? Had he tried to intervene?

"You found her like *what*?" It was almost like Noah was daring him to lie.

Hudson shot to his feet. Liam scrambled up behind him, but Hudson only stretched an arm toward the foyer. "You were there, but go get another look if you're so damn curious."

A fresh torrent of water splashed against the windows hard enough to make me jerk. Sheets of rain began to pound the panes again in a steady onslaught.

Holli leaned back on the sofa and tucked her legs beneath her, seeming to separate herself from the rest of us. "How do you know she was killed?"

Nausea welled in my stomach.

The living room quieted; the only sounds were Aubrey's soft sniffles and the gnashing of too many molars. Holli's shoulders rolled forward. Hiding wouldn't help us now, but I understood the instinct. She added, "I assumed she fell down the stairs. Why do you think it's anyone's fault?"

It was a sane question, a plausible one. The cops—if they were here and taking us seriously—might have asked it.

"The bruises." The answer stuck in my thoughts, holding the rest of my mind hostage. I coughed until my throat eased and I could pretend bile wasn't billowing in my belly. "There were fresh bruises on her wrists."

"She wasn't bruised last night," Hudson offered. He tugged at the fringe at the corner of the throw pillow cradled in his arms.

"That you'd tell us about," Noah shot back. His knee began to bounce double time.

Rory rolled her eyes at their sniping. "What's with you two? Dani's dead and all you can do is have a measuring contest. What gives?"

"Nothing," Hudson muttered.

Noah pushed up from the floor and stalked to the end of the long couch. It put him closest to Dani's body and farthest from Hudson. He didn't glance toward her. I did. That tented sheet failed to fully obscure the image that had already been seared into my brain.

I wrapped my arms around myself and let my fingers fidget against my upper arms.

"She didn't have bruises when I last saw her yesterday. These were dark and circling her wrists. You can look if you want . . ." I trailed off, because I didn't want them to lift that sheet. Dani didn't deserve to be exposed again.

"I heard you last night." Holli scraped her thumbnail across the nail on her ring finger. A fleck of teal peeled away and fluttered to her lap. Then she looked up at Hudson.

Everyone—even Aubrey—gaped at Holli.

If Hudson had turned to stone, he couldn't have been more still.

"Heard who?" This time Noah did look over his shoulder at Dani.

"Hudson and Dani." Holli's voice was even. No accusation pulling her throat tight or fear crunching her words.

Noah snapped his attention back to Hudson. His jaw clenched. Holli began digging at another nail, more polish crinkling up and flaking away. Rory dusted the paint flecks off her girlfriend's leg.

"Why were you fighting?" Holli didn't have to look at Hudson for me to know the question was for him.

Hudson's stuttered "Wh-wh-what are you talking about?" did not bolster any confidence.

Aubrey muffled a soft sob behind her forearm. We'd lost another friend, and the sorrow was fresh and sticky. But if there was a chance to get answers for Dani, I wasn't going to miss it.

Holli must have agreed. She raised her chin, and the fire in her eyes could have razed the room. "I'm talking about you two yelling at each other last night and her storming out on you."

I bit the edge of my tongue to keep from saying anything. I'd planned to keep this secret to test how truthful Hudson was, but now Holli had lit the signal flare. None of us knew what to do with it. The candle on the table flickered, its green wax pouring down its edges and pooling on the glass. The camp light warmed our faces from the other end, but no one spoke. Only the steady *woosha woosha woosha* of water pelting the house filled the room.

"It wasn't like that," Hudson started.

"What *was* it like?" Liam's gentle baritone had hardened.

Defeat warred with disgust in Hudson's sigh, but he answered. "Yes, she left our room in the middle of the night, but she didn't 'storm out.'"

"She slammed a door," Rory prompted.

"I slammed a door, too," he countered, and then caught

himself. He wet his lips, and then continued, "She was upset about Noah."

"Noah? Like that one?" Vic asked, hiking his thumb toward his friend.

Hudson dropped back onto the couch and then tossed the pillow to Liam. "Yes, that one."

Noah leaned forward, elbows on his knees. His face was pulled tight, like sadness and shock had stolen every ounce of ease from his body. "What did I do to her? Because I sure didn't hurt her."

Hudson tripped over his words, but they were filled with pain and confusion, not the violence I would have expected. "You screwed her."

# seventeen

"EXCUSE ME?" Noah settled his weight over his elbows, like he genuinely hadn't heard Hudson accuse him of sleeping with Dani.

"You. Were. Having. Sex. With. My. Girlfriend." Hudson might as well have clapped between each word.

Noah eased back slowly. "I feel like I'd remember that."

"Don't sit here and lie. Not with her behind you."

We were beyond lies. We'd lost two friends in the span of less than a day. *Lost* wasn't even an appropriate word. We'd been robbed. This house—our perfect Jersey Shore escape—had been ransacked for any happiness and our friends' lives had been the pilfered prizes. A chill skated across my lower back.

I pulled the hem of my T-shirt down, as if it would be able to warm me. "Did Dani actually tell you that?"

"Of course she didn't." Noah's pitying gaze was trained on Hudson. Being accused of sleeping with his friend's girlfriend had fully broken Noah out of his catatonic state.

"I saw you." The gravel encasing Hudson's voice hit like

buckshot. He paused for a moment, and this time when he spoke, he sounded completely drained. "I saw them together."

"What exactly did you see?" Liam asked.

"He came out of her room—"

"I live there!"

"What?" Rory leaned forward and took another drink of beer.

I tried to pretend I was surprised, too, still unwilling to admit my eavesdropping.

Noah brushed her off. "Our parents have a thing—you know that."

"Yeah, but not that you were living with Dani." In her shock and anger, even Rory seemed to have forgotten that Dani was lying broken behind us.

"I wasn't 'living with Dani.' Dani and her dad moved in with me and my mom. Our parents are living together. We're just collateral."

*Collateral.* I clenched my jaw.

"When did they move in?" I asked.

He narrowed his gaze at my gentle tone.

I tried again. "Maybe this was a misunderstanding." There was nothing ambiguous about Dani's dead body in the next room, but my heart couldn't take the additional strain of all this fighting.

"A couple months ago."

"And you've been sleeping with her ever since," Hudson snapped.

Holli lifted her gaze from her nails. "Their parents moved in together, dude. Doesn't mean they were shacking up."

"Everyone's looking at me like I'm the asshole." Hudson

tossed his hands up. "I'm not the problem here. I'm the one whose girlfriend was just killed. I'm the one who now has to stare at the guy she was cheating on me with and pretend it isn't a goddamned problem."

"Hud, man—" Liam started.

"No. No. No. I'm not doing this. You want details? You want facts? Fine. I saw him come out of her room half naked just two weeks ago."

A derisive noise shot from the back of Noah's throat and punched through the room. "I live there. Do you always wear a shirt in your house?"

Hudson's lips curled downward until his sneer was dark enough to rival the glowering storm beyond the bay windows. "She was naked in her bed when I walked in."

He wasn't lying. Pain shook his words with such power they should have shattered. He'd found Dani cheating, and hadn't left her. He'd found her naked with another dude leaving her room and had stayed. He'd come to this damn prom house knowing Noah was going to be here. Who did that? Who would put up with that? What did he have to gain by being here with Noah?

"You're awful quiet now, bean pole," Hudson taunted Noah.

If the jab hit, Noah didn't show it. His face had hardened into a stoic mask. No emotion. He might not have even blinked. A loose tendril of hair traced his cheek and jaw.

Liam's soft eyes watched his friend's statue-like stoicism with wariness. He pulled a knee up onto the couch and turned to fully face Hudson. "Why didn't you break up with her?"

"What?" Hudson was watching Noah with hawkish eyes.

"You say you found them sleeping together. I mean, man,

you just told this whole room that you caught your girlfriend cheating on you two weeks ago. Why didn't you ditch her ass?"

Holli and Aubrey let out twin gasps.

I winced. "Really?" Dani was my friend and her corpse wasn't even cold. A little kindness was required.

"Sorry." Liam's voice rang with sincerity, but I saw more to him now. The harsher edges, the recklessness. He'd jumped off the roof with Noah earlier. Maybe he wasn't as thoughtful as I wanted to believe. He focused on Hudson again and rephrased his question. "Why stay with her?"

"Because I love her."

Maybe it was the directness that made me believe him.

Noah's shoulders bobbed in an almost shrug. "And it had nothing to do with you wanting me to hear you two having sex?"

Rory slapped Noah's arm. He jerked away from her.

Cartoon steam should have shot from Hudson's ears. His cheeks turned blood-red. "You can't help yourself, can you?"

"Seriously, Noah?" I whispered. Tension clogged the air; I could barely breathe.

"It's not like we wanted this," he said quickly.

Everyone scoffed at that, even me. "We didn't." His protests grew louder with each word. "She was going to be my sister."

Liam squeezed the back of his neck. "That does not make it better."

"I can't really improve the situation," Noah said.

Even in the low light, Rory's scowl was menacing. "You didn't have to lie to everyone."

Noah's spine snapped straight, like he'd been dunked in ice water. "Right, because telling everyone I was smashing my soon-to-be stepsister was going to go over great. Should I have told her boyfriend first?"

"You could have ended it." There was a wishful plea in Hudson's defeated reply, and I couldn't help but agree.

The bigger problem here was that Dani was dead.

"It doesn't matter who she slept with," I said.

"Maybe not to you," Hudson muttered.

I bit the inside of my cheek until the pain distracted me from the overwhelming roar that had taken up residence in my head. Everyone was throwing accusations, jumping in on the gossip. Even gentle Holli. And I was over all of it.

Our friend was dead in the foyer—the second friend killed—and they were hung up on who'd touched whose goodies.

"Dani didn't trip on the stairs," I said.

"Are you sure?" Vic asked. He'd been quiet during the sex talk, but his hands were fidgeting in the front pocket of his hoodie.

"Those bruised wrists say someone held her." My stomach clenched, but this felt right. I knew I was right. "Someone killed her."

Hudson nodded. "Someone killed my Dani."

"Are you saying . . ." Aubrey's reedy soprano cut through the room. She paused to regroup, gulping back sobs. "Are you saying the person who killed Cam might have killed Dani, too?"

All the agony and grief I'd wedged deep down inside of me began to writhe. Who else was going to be taken from us? Fear slashed at me and burned with each breath. Dani should still be here. We'd missed something. I'd missed something.

"I'm saying we were wrong. The killer is in this room."

# eighteen

IT SAID something about how shell-shocked we all were that no one protested. Sage-green candle wax dripped onto the rug with muffled plops. My boyfriend's lips were parted, and in the dull orange glow of candlelight, I could imagine his exhale of disbelief catching the fire.

My friends' startled gasps reshaped the room. They stretched to the corners of the house and slipped above the still blades of the ceiling fan. I'd spat the truth out in the open, and that brazen act had choked all responses.

Was that a good thing? Once I'd tottered home drunk and Dad caught me. I'd given him a very detailed story about where I'd been and how I could not have possibly ever ingested such an evil elixir as alcohol. It had seemed like a good idea at the time.

Lies were big. They billowed and bloomed in the available space.

A heavy boom resounded to my left. The windows rattled. An uprooted speed limit sign clapped against the glass. The black graffiti in the lower corner was illegible but familiar. It scraped down across the glass, making a horrifying screech. Rory scrabbled away from the window, knocking into the heavy coffee table. Aubrey, Vic, and Holli covered their ears. The roar of the storm ebbed, and the sign fell away from the window.

There was a small, persistent hiss. I could only stare at the crack in the glass.

Rory tracked my gaze. "We need to get out of here."

"We're fine," Noah said automatically.

Vic backpedaled until his shoulders hit a chair, and then he pushed up to sit in it. "Kylie just accused one of us of being a murderer. I'm nowhere near fine."

"She didn't say that." Liam jumping to my defense should have warmed me. The taste of him still clung to my lips, the faint buzz from his kisses last night still lingering.

"I—" I tried to deny it, but that was exactly what I'd said. It was exactly what I'd meant.

I scanned the room, looking for anything to prove me wrong. Some obvious evidence there'd been an intruder. I'd never wanted a person to break into my house, but today that news would have been great.

There were tears in Rory's eyes. Holli's arms were wrapped tight around her torso, her hands disappearing into the extra-long sleeves of her pullover. Hudson's icy visage was trained on his hands. He twirled a ring hanging from a chain around his neck. *Dani's?* One after another, as I looked around the living room, I found worried faces and anxious twitches. Everyone was as freaked as me. Noah and Liam, though? They'd relaxed into mirror positions. Elbows on their knees, like this was a game-day huddle. Like our friends hadn't just been murdered.

Any of them could have done this. The realization chilled

my bones. Hudson had fought with Dani. Noah had loomed over her body. Rory had hated Cam. Aubrey had been sick of his ditching and drinking. Even Liam was big enough to have been able to take Cam down. Holli and Vic were unknowns in comparison. Someone in this room was a murderer, and I had no clue who they were or why they'd kill their own friends.

I walked to the windows. Water lapped at the stairs leading up to the porch, but the flooding wasn't so bad that we needed to try to block the doors yet. The power lines no longer sparked. My chest twanged. The water would still be electrified, though it was hard to say if the whole thing was zap-worthy. Would Hudson try to make another run for it?

I believed him when he said that he hadn't murdered Dani, but then who had? No one could wade through that water to come into this house. My gut began to whirl, like the eddies that had to be churning just offshore.

"Kylie?" Liam's hand was heavy on my shoulder.

"Sorry." I wasn't sure if my apology was for him or for my friends.

He gave me a quick squeeze.

I needed to get to the bottom of this as soon as possible. I couldn't stand being in the presence of a killer, and I didn't even know which person that was. And, well, I was keenly in-terested in not dying. Two people were already gone. A frigid chill cupped the base of my neck and coursed down my spine.

If we didn't out the killer soon, another person I loved would die.

"I know it's a head trip," I said, mostly for myself, "but someone in this room killed Dani. There's no way to get into the house right now, and I refuse to believe those bruises are from anything other than someone grabbing her."

Vic piped up. "Maybe they're from a sex thing?"

Hudson shot to his feet and cleared the few feet between them in the span of a breath. His fist shot forward and cracked against Vic's mouth. Hudson turned his back on the younger guy and strode back to his spot on the couch. "Fuck you."

Vic held a hand up to his split lip, the blood already trickling down his chin.

"Is that a no?" he mumbled.

Hudson sat, content to watch Vic pull up his black shirt to catch the blood pouring from his mouth. "That's a no."

"Punching people is your go-to move, huh? Did you deck Dani, too?" Noah sneered.

Hudson's nostrils flared, but he didn't dole out another fist for Noah.

I had to believe these dick moves were their way of dealing with stress, because otherwise they could all hop in our de facto moat. "Anyone care to share anything? What do we know?"

It seemed like a fair enough place to start.

"You want us to help you figure out if we killed Dani?" Holli asked. She shivered despite the balmy temperature of the living room.

"If you didn't kill her, then you should want to help." The answer was automatic, but the default accusation sparked like a live wire.

"You can't just accuse people," Rory snapped.

"I didn't, but she should want to help."

Holli parted her lips, but Rory was already on it. "Who says you didn't kill her? Want to tell me why you're so calm, so damn motivated to make us answer you?"

"Calm?" Panic scraped my words. "We need answers. We need to know who is doing this. I don't want to be the next person to die, Rory. Do you?"

Rory thrust her palms against the coffee table. It skidded several inches away. The candles and camp light toppled over, dousing the pinprick flames. The dim glow of daylight behind the storm didn't stretch deep into the room, leaving us in only the small glow of the sideways lantern.

Rory's eyes were in shadow, but her dark brows slashed down. "Is that a threat? Because I have no problem taking out any of you who think you can come for me or my girlfriend. I'm not ending up with glass in my neck or my brain bashed in."

She lifted an empty bottle from the floor and held it forward like its round edges were a dagger.

Holli stood and laid a placating hand on her girlfriend's arm.

"I'm fine." She gently pulled the bottle from Rory's hand. "Kylie wants to help us figure this out. Talking is going to keep us safe."

Rory tugged Holli into a protective hug and the two collapsed back onto the couch. My skin shrank beneath her stink eye. I shivered and turned toward Liam. Bewilderment clouded his light eyes, and I wanted to lean into his side. I couldn't do that now, though.

We were falling apart. The wind whistling past the broken glass reminded me we weren't alone. The storm was pressing in on us, and the house was already cracking. How long until someone inside broke, too? How long until I had to see another of my friends' lifeblood pouring into the ground? Bile burned the back of my throat. I welcomed it; this was better than hiding.

I scanned the room again, doing my damnedest to avoid looking toward the foyer and failing when I peered toward Noah. He watched the peaked sheet covering Dani's body from over his shoulder. His jaw was locked, his toes digging into the carpet. *Maybe not so casual.*

This situation was raw clay. I needed to stay easy on the pedal, keep my fingers loose, until whatever happened here— whoever had happened to us—began to take form.

"The person who did that do Dani." Aubrey's voice broke through the silence. She met my gaze. "They did the same thing to Cam."

"We don't know that," Holli said. "Dani fell—or was *maybe* pushed—down a flight of stairs. Cam was stabbed in the neck. They're totally different MOs, if they even were murdered."

Hudson lowered his chin for a moment, and then lifted it as if to defy the room. "The odds of a random killer stab-bing Cam and another murderer taking out Dani? No. I don't buy it."

I didn't either.

"Who would want to kill either of them?" I hadn't meant to ask the question aloud. Suddenly every person found the rug or the mantel or the schooner painting on the far wall incred-ibly interesting. Anything other than looking at their friends.

I squeezed Liam's hand, needing the lifeline. I hadn't meant it as a prompt, but his somber words flowed easily. "I wish I knew. There's no reason for them to not be here right now."

Aubrey nodded and stood. "Kylie's right. We need to talk through this. Who else had been to the firepit with Cam?"

That was as good a place to start as any. The wind hissed through the crack in the window.

Noah wrapped his hair around his fingers and then unwound it again. "We need to cover that window."

Aubrey loomed over Noah, her running shorts making her legs triple in length. "Why are you changing the subject?"

He shook his head. "That pane is going to shatter soon, and we've already lost too much this weekend. We need to board it up before the storm blows in."

"There were a couple empty cardboard boxes in the pantry next to the coolers, I think." Rory was already getting off the couch.

Ten minutes later the window was patched with two Amazon boxes and too much duct tape. I'd found a notebook and pen in the junk drawer and was ready to take notes. I sketched before every art project. This could be like that, I told myself. As if finding a murderer could be as simple as pulling soft sketch lines to set structure for a sculpture.

Liam and I wedged ourselves on the love seat with Hudson. Vic was swallowed by the overstuffed chair, but I could tell from his stricken face that he was going to take this seriously. It was Aubrey, though, at the center of the longer couch, who wanted to run the show.

"So, who was out at the firepit with Cam?" Her question cracked louder than any thunder I'd heard this weekend.

No one spoke.

"Anyone?" she prodded.

This wasn't going to work. We couldn't accuse everyone in the house and expect to get answers. This couldn't become a fight to the death where we all defended only ourselves. Vines of doubt snaked up my ribs.

"Maybe we should figure out how Cam ended up down there," I offered.

"That's what I'm trying to do," she shot back.

Big breath. "Let's just start a little earlier." Placating tones came easily to me. I just mimicked my freshman year art teacher. "When did you last see Cam?"

"Me?" Aubrey asked like I'd accused her of murder.

"Sure." I shrugged. "We can figure out where he went if we all share the last time we saw him." I held the notebook up and waggled it. Might as well get this started. "What about you, Holli?"

"I don't know." If she gnawed her lip any longer, it was going to be bloody. "Probably right when we got back from prom."

Aubrey's scoff was harsh, especially given that she'd lost sight of him, too. "It's not that big of a house. How did you go a couple hours without seeing him?"

"We were"—Holli cast a sidelong glance at Rory—"otherwise engaged."

"For two hours?" Hudson almost smiled.

"Quit picturing it." Rory didn't bother with menace. Not for Hudson. "We were in the pool with you, jackass, probably an hour after that."

She paused, and then nodded toward the notebook in my palm. "And for the record, I didn't see Cam out by the pool while we were swimming, but I was playing some pool polo with Hudson and Dani." Her bravado faltered, and I could hear her sharp intake of breath. It was the most vulnerable I'd seen her yet.

I worked my way around the room, each person giving a begrudging answer about their final encounters with Cam. In the kitchen charging his phone. On the back patio grabbing a beer. Noah had even last run into him exiting the downstairs bathroom.

Finally we came to Vic, the youngest of our group and the person I knew the least. His pouf of curly hair had gained volume overnight, but all of it was directed upward. It didn't add to his stature so much as distract from the zit growing on his chin, red even in candlelight.

"Your turn, Vic," I prompted, pen ready.

"Well . . . he . . . I . . ." He faltered.

"C'mon, man," Noah said, not bothering to hide the fact he wanted this to be over.

I doodled a small diamond in the top corner of the paper and traced the lines a few times. These answers hadn't given me enough yet. Would the killer actually say what I needed to figure this out?

"Fine." Vic was already shaking his head, like the story was too much. "I tried to talk to him out on the pool deck. He jacked the bottle of tequila I brought right out of my hand and told me to screw off."

My hand froze where I'd been doodling on my notebook paper. Why hadn't he mentioned this earlier? Vic wasn't a big dude, but he hadn't stripped to shorts for the pool. Maybe he was hiding some upper-body strength under that video-game T-shirt. Enough to get the drop on Cam? The hummingbird pace of my heartbeat fluttered in my ears.

I couldn't hold back entirely. "And you just let him go?"

"Yeah." Like it was the obvious move. "Wouldn't you?"

"No. We're at a party together," Aubrey snapped.

"Anyone steals my booze, I'm stopping them." Rory's grumble was half-hearted. Her shoulders rolled forward, like she was ready to fold in on herself.

"I wasn't going to fight the guy over a bottle when there were more in the kitchen." Vic made sense, and I hated that he made sense. It didn't change the fact that he'd been the last person to see Cam alive. That he'd been holding what would become the murder weapon.

"Where were you after he took your tequila?" I asked.

"I went to find Noah . . ." Vic's face pinched like he'd knocked back the cheap bourbon without a chaser. "Hey, you didn't ask them that question. I didn't kill him." He held up his open palms like they'd reveal the truth. "Do these hands look like they could kill?"

"What are killer hands supposed to look like?" I asked.

"I don't freaking know, but not this." He shook his hands like he could make us believe him just by waving hard enough.

"Vic didn't kill anyone." Noah spoke softly, but I didn't miss a word. "He's not the type."

Hudson crinkled a plastic water bottle in his hand, each little pop making me want to jump. "Well, one of us is. Some-one killed my girlfriend. And Cam. Are you confessing?"

"You can call her by her name, you know," Noah growled.

"You could have kept your pants on around her."

"You could have broken up with her."

"You both could remember that our friends are dead!" I hadn't meant to shout, but the words released a tight band around my chest. They both shut their mouths, and I sucked in a staggering breath.

Hudson sighed. "I can't stay here."

"We've been through this. We're stuck here until the storm clears and the power lines are dealt with." Fatigue pulled Liam into a slouch beside me.

"Not that." Hudson went quiet, and I thought he might not explain. Maybe we'd already done too much of that today. Then he glanced over at Dani's shrouded form. "We can't keep talking about this in front of her."

# nineteen

RELOCATING DANI wasn't a simple task. We were effectively locked in the house. The kitchen door whined beneath the storm's attention, but we had a corpse to move and nowhere to take her.

"She's asleep," Holli offered. "Put her in a bed."

"She can take mine," Liam said, like Dani needed space from boyfriend drama. I had to hope that wasn't what actually drove her from this world, because of all the ways to go out? Dude drama was royally unfair.

"We can't just *leave* her somewhere." Aubrey's words stretched close to a screech.

"We shouldn't be moving her at all," Rory said, pressing her palm to her face like she couldn't bear seeing us right now.

"She needs to be somewhere safe." Hudson was resolute.

"You don't touch crime scenes, idiot," Rory said. "The cops didn't believe us because Cam was gone. How does moving Dani help her?"

"She'll be protected away from the front door," Hudson countered.

"We mess with the crime scene, we ruin our chances at catching the person who goddamn did this. That what you want? Do you want us to move her because you have something to hide?"

Rory moved closer to Hudson with each word until she stood toe-to-toe with him. It didn't matter that Hudson was double her size. The fire snapping in Rory's eyes said she'd burn him down.

"Maybe she's right." I edged closer. "We could go to one of the bedrooms."

Hudson didn't take his eyes off Rory. "I'm not waiting out this storm holed up in a bedroom with all of you while my girlfriend is alone by the front door."

It was Holli's gentle touch that got Rory to back away. "We're putting her somewhere safe."

"Fine, but for the record, I think it's a bad idea," Rory muttered before easing away from Hudson.

I let out a long breath. We shouldn't have to be dealing with how to handle dead bodies. We shouldn't have to be questioning our friends. I shouldn't be standing here wondering about crime scene contamination and measuring who was most comfortable around the dead.

"What if she disappears?" Aubrey asked.

My lungs locked for a long moment. Cam's body was gone. Dani vanishing was a risk.

"The doors are bolted and the storm is holding us in here," Noah offered softly.

Liam nodded. "He's right. If we can't get out, then she can't go anywhere." I appreciated that he didn't call Dani a corpse.

I pulled in two heavy breaths before agreeing with the guys. "She'll be safe in Liam's room, Aub."

I hoped I was right.

Liam and Hudson tucked the edges of the sheet around her body, and then tried to make quick work of moving her. *Tried* being the operative word. Moving a dead body was absolutely as awkward as it looked on TV. Both guys struggled with the unwieldy deadweight. Noah hustled forward to help.

"Not you," Hudson bit out. He adjusted his grip on his girlfriend's shoulders and then inclined his chin toward Vic. "You."

The three of them shuffle-stepped their way up the stairs, carefully cradling Dani's body. Once they laid her in the bed that was supposed to be Liam's, Hudson tucked blankets around her and then gently closed the door behind him on their way out, like the snick of the latch would wake her. The hallway was overwhelmed with silence. Winston was still battering the outside of the house, probably hovering over the coast like a squatter, but our fighting had been exhausted, at least for the moment.

That left us with our grief.

It left me with my guilt.

How many stairs had she tumbled down before she'd broken the first bone? The second? Her neck?

Could I have stopped this?

"I can't stand this," Rory said.

Vic was less caustic than usual. "Which part?"

"All of it? The waiting, the death, the standing here doing jack-all." I almost thought tears glistened at the edges of her eyelids, but it had to be a trick of the newly lit candle she was now cradling.

"As long as we stay together, we'll be fine." There was a surety Noah possessed that I envied.

I wanted his confidence that this would work out. That the remaining eight of us could walk out of this house unscathed—or, at least, no more so than we already were.

"Not if she's right." Vic jerked a thumb toward me. "If she's right, then someone in this hallway is a murderer and we're all potential victims."

"I didn't say that." At least not all of it.

"So the inquisition earlier was for giggles?" Vic took two steps toward me. He wasn't taller than me, but his heavy breathing pushed his chest forward like a pigeon puffing up to clean its feathers.

"I just want everyone to be safe." It was the truth.

Aubrey was less cautious. "She didn't say more people are getting murdered, but someone here is a killer, and there *will* be justice."

Her gangly frame looked leaner, meaner in this moment, her cheeks darkening.

"Once we can get out of here, the cops can help us." Liam was being reasonable. Sound and steady. It should have soothed me, but there was now a body in his bed and his reaction to finding Dani was still seared to the backs of my eyelids. I tried to shake the thought. There was no reason to doubt him. The stress, the horror, the bone-breaking sadness baked into this night/morning/weekend—it was all getting to me.

Focus on the process.

I could hear my pottery teacher in my head. *Take the steps and the creativity will come.* I nodded. I didn't need to design anything momentous right now, but I needed to let the truth bubble its way up. Process. Yes. I nodded again.

"Let's take a breath, and then we can talk more about what happened to both of our friends."

Aubrey had pushed us to focus on Cam, but maybe Dani's death was the key to figuring this out. Who had been awake with her? Who would want to hurt her? Who had seen them both?

I needed time to map out the notes from earlier.

Aubrey's stomach growled. She quickly muttered, "Sorry."

"I could eat, too," Noah said, giving her a one-armed hug.

"Of course you could eat after this," Hudson said.

"We can see what survived in the kitchen," I said, and then tacked on, "together."

Liam nodded like a military captain. "No one breaks off alone."

"What about the bathroom?" Rory asked, punching up the petulance in her question.

"Girls go to the bathroom together all the time," Liam replied with a snicker.

I smacked Liam's arm. "Sticking together is good."

As long as we weren't sticking with the person who had no problem shoving a shard of glass in someone's neck or tossing a friend down the stairs.

My mom preached that adulthood was all about making good choices. Not everything was in your control, though. My friends were good people. They always had been. But if that were true, then how were two dead and another their likely killer? What had I overlooked? Whatever it was, I hoped it didn't get me killed.

# twenty

THE LIVING room became our de facto home base. It was the room that could hold us all, and somehow the cluster of candles on the coffee table had given me hope that we could push away the darkness while we figured a way out of this.

I shouldn't have fallen asleep. I shouldn't have been *able* to fall asleep, but we were all just so exhausted by this point. As I woke, I rubbed my knuckle against the corner of my eye, ignoring the smudges of black from my forgotten mascara that now marred my finger.

The waxy flames had slipped low. My notebook was flopped open against my chest. I prodded the cushion on either side of me and found the pen dipped against the rolled edge of fabric. I tucked it into the metal coils binding the notebook and then stretched my arms overhead. My right shoulder popped.

Liam wasn't there. He wasn't on the far couch where Rory and Holli slept in a pile. He wasn't tucked at a dining room chair scowling at Scrabble tiles with Aubrey, Hudson, and Vic. Noah wasn't here either, but the fact that Liam and Noah tended to do everything together didn't comfort me.

I padded toward the kitchen, my bare feet treading on the hardwood floors as lightly as possible. I'd agreed we shouldn't go anywhere alone. When we'd been separated from one another, our friends had died. I paused at the doorway, looking back at my sleeping friends and the ones playing the only board game we could find in the house. They hadn't noticed me leaving the room. How long would it take them to realize I was gone? How long had Cam been out at that firepit before Aubrey and I had found him? How long had he been there before the killer had sought him out? And Dani? My throat squeezed.

No, I wasn't going to skip out of eyesight alone. I couldn't do that, even for Liam.

I gripped the door frame and then leaned into the kitchen. If only my head and shoulders left the room, it didn't count, right? It also kept the walls from creeping in on me. I hadn't carried a candle or a camp lantern with me, and the kitchen had disappeared into inky shadows and sooty corners. Plenty of space for secrets.

Secrets, but not Liam. If he were in here, there'd be a light. There'd be a voice. Some sound stretching from the sheer darkness, but all I heard were the steady sounds of the sturdy home moaning against the storm.

I pulled myself back into the living room. After making my way back to the couch, I picked up the notebook and reread my notes, like they'd distract me from the fact that Liam wasn't here right now. I still didn't know who killed Dani and Cam, but I was certain it was someone in this house. Vic had seen Cam before Noah and Liam had done their rooftop leap into the pool. My mental math skills weren't perfect, but I knew that meant Cam couldn't have been throwing back shots solo for multiple hours. It had to have been thirty minutes at most.

The image of the vibrant blood seeping beneath his shirt rose sharp behind my eyes, and my stomach swelled with sickness.

Cam's drinking situation wasn't supposed to be public knowledge, but how many of us had known? It was the cause of most of his and Aubrey's breakups. I knew. Rory knew, which meant Holli probably knew. Did the guys know? Would Cam have confided in Hudson or Liam? Who else would have known he'd probably slink off at a party to drink alone? Did that mean it had to be one of the girls in the house? Aubrey had been shattered when we'd found him. She'd been with me beforehand, too.

No, I tried to shake the possibility from my mind. Not Aubrey.

Did that mean it was Rory? Who I'd known since I was little? Who I had played volleyball with for the whopping three years when I had pretended I was athletic in middle school? Who had let me practice driving her car when my parents kept avoiding the issue by saying, "You're just going to take the subway in the city anyway"?

Adrenaline shifted to sludge in my veins.

I stretched my fingers before flipping the page in the notebook. I already knew what was on the next page. Dani and Noah were an unofficial side thing. A soon-to-be-sibling side thing.

And Hudson had found out. Only I didn't doubt him. He loved her, but he was also the most averse to change of any of us. He'd stayed with her to avoid that conflict. For a guy who loved physical clashes, he was ill-equipped when it came to emotional entanglements. Yes, he'd managed to call her out on it—kind of—last night; I'd heard their fight. But the chance of losing her completely? I didn't buy that he'd go there.

Maybe if I didn't know them, I would have been able to see it that way. Hell, maybe I *should* be seeing it that way. My gut said it wasn't Hudson. Which left me with . . . *what?* A whole lot of notes about who was where and some facts about who was sleeping with whom. And no answers about who had murdered my friends or why.

What I did know was my boyfriend still wasn't with the group. It'd been long enough by now that if he and Noah had ducked out for the restroom, they would have already returned.

Liam was missing.

Like Cam had been.

He had disappeared like Dani. And just like Hudson, I'd been asleep when he had vanished. I wouldn't be able to handle finding his body. I wouldn't *accept* the possibility of finding Liam broken or bleeding.

I couldn't wait any longer. We needed to find Liam and Noah. Risking losing another person—possibly my person— wasn't an option.

My voice shook as I echoed the question Aubrey had asked me just minutes before we found her boyfriend with a bit of a broken liquor bottle jutting from his neck: "Have you seen Liam?"

# twenty-one

NO ONE remembered when Liam and Noah had left. Did that mean they'd recently left and I'd missed it? Maybe my timing was off and they'd barrel back in from the downstairs bathroom. But the ice in my bones said otherwise.

"We need to find them." I was sticking to this confident, crime-solving character I'd stepped into, even if my voice couldn't catch a steady note.

Aubrey's full lips—no liner needed—had paled. "Let's go."

Vic pushed up from the table first, Hudson a half second behind. A flash of warmth pulsed with my heart, but only for a single beat. I wasn't alone. But if all three came with me, who would protect Holli and Rory?

I held up a hand. "What about them?"

"They're together," Vic said automatically.

"They're *asleep,*" Aubrey's response was equally immediate. Vic's biggest concern about falling asleep at a party involved phallic Sharpie scrawling on his face. Ours was much scarier.

His brows furrowed. "They aren't going anywhere."

We'd clearly been taught different lessons. If they were both asleep, they weren't safe. Leaving them unguarded wasn't the kind of chance we took on a normal night, and this was far from a normal night. "We need to wake them."

Aubrey started toward them before I could, but Hudson stopped her with a bulky hand on her shoulder.

"I'll stay here." There was kindness in his heavy words. And something sharper, sadder beneath them.

I hesitated. Our sleeping friends wouldn't be alone, but was Hudson the right person to stay with them? He'd fought with Dani before she died. I'd watched him punch Vic in the face, and it sure seemed like he'd done the same to Noah.

"I should probably stay, too." Aubrey's offer was soft, but the strain beneath it said she'd reached the same conclusion: Hudson might be the killer.

He rolled his eyes. "It doesn't take two of us to watch them sleep."

Hudson was more than a wild card. He could be dangerous, and if that were true, he could have easily killed Dani. He was big enough to take out Cam. Holli and Rory would be easy targets alone with him.

I nodded slowly. "Maybe she's right. Then you're alone on guard duty."

Hudson winced. My excuse of having Aubrey there for his protection sounded weak even to my ears. "The longer we stand here, the longer we don't know what's happening to Liam." The flat line of his lips said he'd left Noah out of consideration on purpose.

"He's got it, guys," Vic said. "Or am I going to have to volunteer to stay down here now, too?"

"It'll be fine." Hudson cast a sidelong peek at the stairwell.

He didn't want to go back to where he'd last seen Dani. Where he'd last seen her both alive and dead. I knew it as firmly as I knew there was a killer in this house.

"Okay." I nodded to him in thanks. I had to hope I wasn't wrong about Hudson, had to hope he hadn't hurt our friends.

I lingered at the base of the stairs. Even without a candle or lantern to illuminate the room, I could imagine the blood soaked into the foyer rug mere feet from me. My stomach soured. This rental house might be picture-perfect, but there were already too many spots soaked in misery for me. I gritted my teeth and quickly stepped around the rug.

Vic took the first couple steps two at a time. He didn't notice the photograph of long woman watching him at the landing. I averted my gaze from the picture, not willing to catch her eye, and took in a print of the New York skyline at sunrise. The water was calm and shimmered with pinks and oranges. Nothing like the black and blue bruises eddying off the Jersey Shore now.

The floorboard beneath my feet groaned as I took the first step, and then suddenly Aubrey was at my side. She laced her fingers with mine. The sloppy bun atop her head had slipped down to the right. She looked drunkenly disheveled without even having knocked back a drink. I gave her hand a quick squeeze. Her golden heart ring bit at my middle finger. I welcomed the grounding pain and started up the stairs again.

The walls weren't rattling here. Had the storm quelled, or was it all in my head? The steps whined with our progress. Had they been this loud earlier? Had Dani heard me clomp down them? Sand ground against the ball of my foot on several of the steps, and the memory of what our weekend beach trip should have been like tugged at me, but I kept moving forward. It's all I could do now.

Vic leaned over the railing from the second floor. His curly hair cascaded around his face like a mane. "Are we sure they're up here?"

"Where else would they be?" Aubrey asked.

Playing worst-case scenario wasn't going to improve the aching worry in my rib cage.

"They weren't in the kitchen," I reminded them. That would stop them from wandering down this path of conversation, right?

"Yeah." Vic stretched the word out. He'd brought one of the lanterns and it swung over the railing like a beacon on a ship's bow—shaky, but enough to light the way. "But what if they were somewhere else down there?"

"Then we'll look there next," I snapped.

Aubrey and I rounded the stairs onto the landing. She pressed her shoulder against mine, bracing me.

"This isn't like before," she whispered.

I needed her to be right. Dread had seeped into my belly. The panicked whirl of *he could be dead, he could have disappeared, he could be gone* echoed against my skull. Pounding and pounding.

This hallway looked the same as it had when I'd tiptoed past it early in the morning. There wasn't even sand on the floor here. All the doors were closed save the bathroom at the far end. The darkness was deeper past the ajar door, but as we edged into the hallway, flashes of the white and blue tile lining the floor and walls behind the toilet were caught in Vic's swinging light.

I listened for voices, but there was nothing but the squeak of an aging plank beneath my right foot and Vic's huffing breath.

He didn't hesitate, I'll give him that. Vic's pathetic jokes hadn't won me over, but he flung open the door to what had been Hudson and Dani's room like he had no doubt it'd be empty. Like he had no fear of finding our friends' bodies. Did he have more faith in them, or had he simply not been as irrevocably shaken by seeing their corpses as I had been?

Aubrey and I shuttled in behind him. Big, tufted pillows littered the floor, the rumpled sheets were thrown back on the bed, and an oversized, yellow duffel bag was wedged on a vanity stool, gym shorts spilling out. Aubrey cautiously pulled open the closet door, but no skeletons fell forward.

My sigh of relief was audible. Both Aubrey and Vic shot me a look.

Vic grinned. "They're probably trying to find us a better game than Scrabble."

"You just don't like it because you're a crappy speller." Aubrey wrapped her arms around herself.

"Wollor *is* a word," he muttered.

"Would they be in your room, then?" I asked Vic because I had to, not because I wanted to.

"We can't go in there." Aubrey's words rang with finality.

Dani was in Noah, Liam, and Vic's room. We couldn't go back to her. Opening that door was more than forcing ourselves to look at her body again, barely concealed by a sheet. It was cracking the lid on my fear. It was breaking the temporary seal on Aubrey's sanity. Overflowing grief and anguish wouldn't help us now. We had to keep it locked tight, and that meant staying out of Vic's room.

"We *can* go in there . . ." He trailed off when he met Aubrey's wild gaze. I ground my teeth together like it would keep me from crying. It worked, but just barely.

"Or not." He retreated to the doorway, too.

We checked Holli and Rory's room next. I stubbed my toe on the foosball table in the corner of the game room at the end of the hallway. Aubrey pushed into the bathroom, Vic hovering at her back with the lantern held high, and me taking up the rear. Vic was shorter than Aubrey but stretched to keep the light overhead. The shower curtain, which was peppered with forget-me-nots, had been pulled closed. Could you taste your own heartbeat? I was pretty sure my pulse had pushed the bitter, acidic flavor of coffee up to my taste buds. Aubrey reached for the curtain, but hesitated.

"Not another body." My lips barely moved. It had been a prayer for me, not meant for Vic's or Aubrey's ears, but I realized too late that they had heard. Aubrey's shoulders hitched up. If she hadn't been thinking it, she was now.

"Oh, come on." Vic stretched forward and whipped the curtain to the right. The reveal was both dramatic and anti-climactic.

Because the basin was bare. Clean, white porcelain looked back at us. Unmarred and unused. There weren't even echoes of hard-water droplets. I swallowed and hoped that the sour espresso taste overwhelming my mouth wasn't about to flip my stomach.

"See? Nothing." Vic swung the lamp over the tub.

I didn't need his showboating. I needed to find my boyfriend and get back to the group. "Yeah, we see."

"Noah's probably done with whatever Boy Scout thing he

was doing and now they're downstairs laughing at us." Vic slid past me out into the hallway.

"You wanted to come with us." Petulance didn't sound good on me, but the lack of a body hadn't calmed my nerves. The fine hairs on my forearms were standing at attention, and with each passing second another worry nipped at my neck.

"I'm here to protect you." His sincerity meant jack-all to me. He had dismissed our worries and blasted forward without thinking. What if there had been a body in that tub? Had he even considered how much worse he could make everything?

"Then help us," Aubrey said simply. The shadows had slipped around her until I could only guess at her profile.

Vic staggered to a stop in the center of the hallway. He still held the camp light overhead. It swayed wildly, alternately illuminating his face and cutting dark ravines across it. The whites of his eyes were vivid regardless.

"Fine." He lowered the lantern to shoulder height. "Then let's get upstairs and get this over with."

Aubrey stepped forward. I exhaled and nodded toward the stairs, and the three of us started up the next flight.

Why would Liam and Noah have gone to the third floor? It was only my room, Aubrey's, and another bathroom. It was spacious, but there weren't board games or books or a surplus of storm supplies. There were just bedrooms.

Beds. My heart slid down my spine.

Beds like the one I'd shared with Liam. Leaden dread encased my ankles. They could be in my room. Would Liam be telling Noah we'd had sex? Had I misjudged him? Were they laughing about it?

I snagged my toe on the rise of a step and tripped forward.

I caught myself on the railing and tried to absorb its steady resolve.

"You good?" Aubrey asked. Our lone lamp was ahead of us, but I didn't need to see her eyes to catch the edge of worry in her whisper.

"Yep." Lying was easier than admitting I was already doubting Liam. He'd thrown up a few caution flags, but did he deserve my suspicion? I pulled a couple slow breaths in through my nose and willed my body to chill out.

The door to my bedroom—our bedroom?—was open. We'd left a candle burning on the nightstand. The wick was fighting to stay lit in the deep pool of melted wax.

Neither Liam nor Noah were inside. I pointed my toe and rolled my ankle. The weight eased, but each step I took toward Aubrey's bedroom door was unsure. Fear made my footsteps cautious, more rock-climbing careful than curfew-breaking creeping.

This was the last bedroom. If they weren't inside, we'd have to go into Noah's bedroom. We'd have to see Dani again. And what if they weren't in there either? Could they have gone outside? A flurry of lightning flickered and flashed outside the window like it'd heard my thoughts.

No, they couldn't have left.

I reached for the doorknob, but I couldn't let myself turn it. The need to find Liam and Noah gripped my throat with an iron fist, but the desire to protect myself—from another dead body, from the possibility my boyfriend either had been murdered or was a murderer, from the heartbreak that might lie on the other side of the door—was choking me from the inside.

The floor groaned behind me. Probably Vic about to be

bossy and push his way ahead again. My irritation at him over-rode my fears for a half second, which was long enough to make me open the door and step through.

Liam was alone. He stood next to the bed, his lips parted in a round O, his eyes wide and fevered.

Blood smeared his forehead.

"Kylie." My name stretched from his mouth like we were miles apart instead of mere feet.

He reached for me with blood-soaked hands.

# twenty-two

MY SCREAM scared even the storm into silence. The walls didn't dare to shake. The thunder eased to a sputtering cough. Even the wind paused its whistle.

Or maybe I was just that damn loud.

"I—I—I—" Liam tried.

Tears burned my eyes.

Liam stopped just in front of me, his bloody hands falling down by his sides. I stepped back out of arm's reach.

"It's not what you think," he said in a jumbled rush. A half-burned candle flickered on a far dresser, and there was a lantern to Liam's right. When he turned toward me, the blood streaking his forehead looked black as night.

My teeth started to chatter, but I gritted them. "It looks like you're covered in blood."

He didn't have any visible wounds. No gash was gushing at his hairline. The blood was static, necrotic, and damning.

Vic and Aubrey flanked my sides.

"It's—" Liam started again.

"What happened to you?" Vic asked, like my boyfriend was covered in mud and not someone else's bodily fluids.

Liam lowered his hands. In the light of Vic's lamp, the blood on his forehead had turned red again, but his olive skin looked sickly green. "That's what I was trying to explain."

I couldn't release my jaw yet, but I also couldn't hold back the question. "Whose blood is that?"

Wearing evidence on your face like this had to be the number one way for killers to get caught.

He narrowed his eyes at me. Hurt flashed within them.

"Come see for yourself." He pressed a hand to his eye, and then stopped when he realized he had smeared more blood on his face. "Sorry. No. Don't. This is—" A heavy sound wedged in his throat. He coughed against it, the fake kind that buys time. "I don't want you to have to see him, too."

The kiln burning bright inside me began to cool. "Who?"

Aubrey's cry hitched in her chest. She hiccuped on sobs and pressed her hand to her mouth as if she could stop them. I understood the feeling. It felt like my emotions were being tossed to sea and crashing against the stones just offshore. Each time I'd thought I'd successfully hauled them back inland, the tide reeled them back to sea.

Only Aubrey's gaze wasn't locked on my bloody boyfriend. She'd found hers.

Cam's navy-blue Top-Siders were a muted gray in the dim room. His feet poked past the edge of the closet door. His ankles were swollen and the skin sallow. I was thankful the rest of his body was behind the partition. The sight of the stabs and slashes was already seared in my mind. I didn't need an additional glimpse.

Aubrey tottered forward carefully, like she was wearing six-inch heels. I stilled her with two fingers on her forearm and breathed, "Don't."

Her earlier determination had seeped away, and she vibrated with fresh sorrow.

"That's what I was trying to warn you about." Liam's stance softened. "We found Cam."

*We.* Liam was alone in this room when we'd walked in. "Where's Noah?"

"Here."

I jumped at the booming baritone behind me. Noah stood in the doorway holding two tea towels.

"Noah! The shit, man?" Vic clapped his friend on the back, but his laughter was tinged with the truth: He was scared. *About time.*

"There's a bathroom with towels at the end of the hall." He waved his prizes. "Needed to clean up."

There was no terror tainting a single thing Noah said. How had finding a body not rattled him? He'd been broken upon seeing Dani, but seeing Cam's corpse didn't faze him?

"Are you serious?" I tried not to lose it. Really I did.

He tossed a towel to Liam. "Basic protocol. We need to regroup and figure out what to do next."

It was so organized. So strategic. Like he was following some rule book for what to do when you find the corpse of your murdered friend stuffed in a closet.

"Boy Scout." Liam whispered the reminder for my ears, but there were no more secrets to be had in this room. Not with blood on the floor and a body around the corner.

"I'm just happy to know where he is." Relief washed Noah's

face, but he still fisted the cloth in his hand tight enough the veins in his forearm were beginning to pop.

"How long do you think . . . ?" Aubrey trailed off, swallowing a sob.

Noah didn't hold back. "How long was he in there?"

I thought of the sand on the stairs. The blood marring the walls where Dani had fallen. Was that all from her? Had I missed the beach debris in the stairwell earlier because of the chaos or had someone just done this? If so, who?

We'd been together.

All of us.

Hadn't we?

Liam scrubbed his hands against the terry cloth. He didn't move, but his eyes tracked me. I needed out of here, I needed answers, I needed to comfort my boyfriend but wasn't willing to touch him yet, I needed out of this house. I felt like I could barely get enough air into my lungs.

We'd found Cam. That was good, but it only further underscored the fact that the killer was in this house. Why had they hidden him in Aubrey's room? Why had they hidden him at all? The body had already been found. The police had already been called. What was the point of putting him here?

"Why were you up here?" I kept my gaze locked on the four panels of the closet door. It could handle the accusation that had buried itself in my question.

"The lighter we found in the junk drawer was out of fluid." Liam's words were plain, direct, and—I really hoped—honest.

"I had a spare one in my go bag, which I'd dumped up here when we'd crashed out with Aubrey," Noah added.

That shook Aubrey from her shock. "What?"

Oh, right. I forgot that Aubrey had been so out of it, she didn't remember the previous night. "We didn't want anyone to be alone. You were snoozing pretty hard, so Vic and Noah crashed on the floor in here."

"Just to keep you safe," Vic said, like the idea of touching Aubrey disgusted him.

She didn't notice. "On the floor?"

Both guys nodded, and that appeased Aubrey. She turned her attention back to the body of her boyfriend. "Was he here with us? All night?"

She worried at her lower lip and tears welled at the corners of her eyes, but she remained upright. No one answered her. The room hummed with rattled breaths—or maybe that was the window?

"He isn't lost anymore," I said, because at least that was true.

Aubrey wavered on unsteady legs. When I thought she might crumple to the floor, she asked, "What were you going to do with him?"

"That was what we were working on. Cleanup for us, and then we were going to come talk to you guys." Noah eased farther into the room, and somehow I knew he already had a plan for how to handle this. If only he had a plan for finding the killer. That one was still on me, apparently.

Anger pitted in my throat. "Why did you leave without telling anyone? Were you going to move Cam without telling us, too?"

Noah's eyes clouded. "You were asleep."

The accusation beneath the fact dug at me. "Exhaustion will do that, but then someone said we were safe if we stayed together."

Noah's upper lip twitched. "We *are* safer together."

"Noah's right. We should get back downstairs." Vic was already looking to the exit. "We left Hud alone with a couple sleeping girls."

My heartbeat raced. He wasn't accusing Hudson of murder, and yet a tingle raced its way up my spine.

"We can explain everything. Let's just get downstairs." Liam seemed like he was trying to convince himself, and it wasn't working.

I lifted my chin and peered at the unmoving ceiling fan. It offered no advice. Shaking my head didn't clear my mind of this horrifying fog any more than finding Cam's corpse had assuaged my fear that I was bunking with a killer.

"We can't leave him here," I said. It should have been Aubrey refusing to walk away; it was her boyfriend concealed behind the closet door.

Aubrey didn't disagree, but then she wasn't saying anything either. She'd turned toward the window, as if she could see more than a miasma of navy blue and streaky black.

"We need supplies," Noah said with a huff.

Liam shook his head. Was he disagreeing with Noah or me?

I said his name slowly, carefully. He turned to me, lips parted. It was as if he'd forgotten I was in the room. He gripped the towel in his hand tighter, knuckles going red.

"Uh, Liam?" Vic's back was pressed to the door frame, but he was clearly worried about my boyfriend's slackening jaw.

I edged forward and grasped the towel in Liam's hand. "You can let go."

I'd meant the towel, but he leaned forward and dropped his chin onto my shoulder. His arms clasped around my body tight, and I managed not to pull away when his chest rattled against me. He tightened his hold, his strength holding me in place and maybe keeping himself from crumbling in front of our friends.

The invisible thorns that had pricked beneath my skin when we'd first found them up here began to retreat with each steadying breath Liam took. Maybe it was that I couldn't see beyond the cotton fabric of his shirt, but my chest muscles finally began to unlock. Liam's fingers pressed more firmly against my back, and a soft whimper slipped from my mouth.

"Ahem." It might have been Noah or Vic. I didn't know or care.

Until a hard fist collided with my upper arm. "My boyfriend is lying dead ten feet away, and you can't keep your hands off the guy who's covered in his blood?"

# twenty-three

AUBREY HAD punched me.

*For real* punched me.

I released Liam to cup my sore arm and bit the inside of my cheek to keep from spitting sharp barbs her way. She was in pain, I reminded myself. But it didn't soothe the sting.

Liam's right hand still cupped my waist, his fingers pressed so firmly that there'd be red prints later. I wasn't sure if I was his towline or if he was even aware of his grip.

He tilted his chin toward Aubrey. "You aren't the only one grieving, you know."

There was more than grief in this bedroom. The air had thickened with a briny tang, and true terror had begun to cut through it all with an acrid scalpel. My throat burned, and I staggered out of Liam's reach.

"Your girlfriend is right there. So I think my situation is a lot more dire. If she were in Cam's place, you'd get it."

Aubrey might as well have slugged me in the gut. Had she really just said that? Like if I had been murdered, it would have made things fair? A flame kindled behind my breastbone, crackling and gasping for oxygen. Tears fell before I even registered the heat at my eyes. Anger was easier to manage than the slick, coiled terror waking in my belly.

Liam stepped toward her. "You want to take that back?"

Noah edged away from the closet. His shoes left bloody half-circle imprints with each step. "You're really going to threaten her?" he asked Liam.

"He just doesn't want to admit he went after Cam." It was Aubrey's accusation that broke me.

I bent forward, as if folding at the waist would quell the beast raging in my belly. There was more blood on the floor here. I tried to lift my gaze.

Liam hadn't backed down. "You've got to be kidding! We found him in *your room*."

Arms wrapped around my middle, thick bands holding me steady from behind. My chest quaked. Was I sobbing?

"Stay here. It's okay," Vic said at my ear.

Was he yelling? Was I moving? I tried to stagger forward, but Vic's grip was solid.

"What is wrong with you?" My question cracked like a whip through the room. The silence that followed was punctuated only with sharp exhales, everyone trying to catch their breath.

Anger was a race and we were all losing.

"I . . ." Aubrey searched the walls of the room for the right thing to say. Her lips pulled into a perfect pout. She finally settled on "I don't know why I said that."

*Me neither.* Questioning our friendship wasn't the kind of trial I could take this weekend. The one person who should not be on my suspect list was Aubrey. She was the person I could trust with my deepest, darkest secrets. Aubrey was the person who would see my sketches—complete with catawampus reference lines and ghostly scratch marks—and would tell me the piece was going to be gorgeous, even though she had no idea what I'd drawn. She had confidence in me and had watched my back in every situation. Cam had been murdered, I told myself, and it had broken her more severely than it had me. My heart was intact, if not wrapped in necessary razor wire. Giving her a pass on this might hurt, but it was also necessary.

"That's the best you can do?" Liam rallied.

I tapped Vic's bracing arms around my middle, and he released me. Touching Liam didn't soften his rage, but it did get him to step back, closer to me.

"We're all . . ." I couldn't help but peek toward Cam's body. From here I could see the blood on his legs, the splotches on the outside of his Top-Siders. I tried again. "We're all on edge. This room, Cam, all of it. We need to go downstairs and talk this through."

"More talking?" Noah sounded like I was wasting his time.

"She's right. Besides, do you have a better plan?" Aubrey backed me as if her earlier outburst hadn't happened. The rumble of unease in my belly said otherwise.

"We need to assess our supplies, because that storm isn't abating." Noah scrubbed his hands against a towel, though they were free of blood already. "I want to keep everyone here together and safe. I know we're all worried about who's behind this, but I just want to protect everyone instead of pointing fingers at one another."

"I thought you brought a bunch of hurricane gear?" Vic asked.

"Weren't you up here to get supplies anyway?" I added.

Noah held his hands up in surrender. The pale pink towel in his hand marred with bloody streaks didn't help the situation. "I'm trying to keep everyone together and protected, and now you're accusing me of what?" He stared down each of us in turn. "Seriously. What is this?"

"Hey, Noah. Chill. I just meant, what else could we need? You brought the lanterns"—Vic held his aloft—"and the tarp, lighter fluid, rope." I wanted to raise my eyebrows at this list, but I kept my face a mask. "What else do we need?"

Noah's smile spread slowly until his lips were curled in a true grin. "You really haven't ever helped with hurricane prep, have you?"

Vic shrugged.

"More cardboard would be smart. We might look to see if the landlord left anything we could use as sandbags and do a quick check on perishables."

"We aren't going to be here for weeks," I said, willing it to be true.

"No, but the corner-store ice in our coolers isn't going to keep forever, and it's mostly chilling beer." Noah was practical.

Even Aubrey had to nod at that.

"Okay," I said with finality that rang through the room. "We can assess the house and regroup, but then we need to talk about all this."

Noah turned away quickly, but I swear he rolled his eyes.

"Who wants to help me carry Cam?" he asked before

hoisting our dead friend on top of his shoulder in a fireman's carry. Aubrey cried out and covered her eyes. "Someone has to spot me on those stairs."

I hadn't handled Cam's body, but that didn't stop me from staring at my palms, waiting for blood to appear. My hands were clean in the soap-and-water sense, but guilt was sticky even if it wasn't earned. I certainly wasn't a killer, but suspicion was knotting my insides.

Liam tried to pass me a bottle of water, but even the thought of sipping it made my stomach cry out.

They placed Cam in the same bedroom as Dani. It made logical sense, but at some point one of us was going to admit we'd made a temporary morgue in a Shore house. I doubted *that* detail was going to make the future vacation rental listing. No one was going to proclaim the ocean access, the pool, the five expansive bedrooms, and the optional dead-body storage. I sure wouldn't have agreed to the invite if anyone had mentioned that.

Three candles burned in the living room. The golden light wavered from face to face in time with my breathing. Rory and Holli were awake and upright now. Rory's face was drawn, but the dark hollows in her cheeks could have been from lack of sleep or the minimal lighting. I would have gone to her in another situation, offered a hug. But we were all in need of consolation now. We were all suspects. How screwed up was that?

The center flame snuffed out in its own wax. Wind howled outside the front door.

I'd been the one who had said we had to talk this through, like the killer would raise their hand and we'd be able to boot them out into the storm. My friends' faces looked skeletal by this point. Wan cheeks and darkened eyes refused to meet one another. Even Holli and Rory kept a few inches between them. We didn't have to speak the truth to feel it, and the fact was one of us had murdered two of our friends.

"Kylie?" Liam said.

I cleared my throat, and he took it as acknowledgment.

"Can we talk?" he asked.

I should have said no. I should have said we needed to talk with everyone else. I should have stayed on the couch. Instead I nodded. "What's up?" My attempt at acting casual backfired when my voice squeaked.

He hesitated. "Can we go in the kitchen?"

I struggled to stand, like my legs were no longer my own. I was acutely aware that stepping into a side room with my boyfriend—who I'd kind of, sort of implied was a killer—went against the plan of staying together for survival.

I lifted my chin to tell him so to his face. The consternation I found there carried me to my feet. I slipped my hand in his, and we started toward the kitchen.

Aubrey sat on the short sofa, her chin propped on the heel of her hand and her expression empty. I leaned down to her. "Going to check the pantry for provisions with Liam. We'll be right back."

I almost told her to come look for me if we weren't back in ten minutes, but I was supposed to trust him. And her. Both relationships were on shaky ground right now, but I needed them if I was going to get through this.

She waved me away with a "Yeah, fine."

At least one of us was over the exchange upstairs. Spoiler alert: It wasn't me.

Liam plucked a candle from the top of the mantel and lit it on the closest flame. Our tiny torch in hand, we strode into the kitchen.

There was a blackout curtain effect from the storm that threw the kitchen into pitch darkness. It didn't matter that it was technically morning or that the sun was likely creeping overhead. Hurricane Winston didn't care. Liam dropped my hand and lifted the lid of the closest cooler.

"Do you want something to drink? This one's beer." He closed the lid and opened the next one. "Or water?"

I couldn't stomach the idea of either. "I'm good."

He pulled a fresh bottle of water from the second cooler, cracked the cap, and took a long drink.

"So." I swallowed hard. "What did you want to talk about?"

I knew, but there was a difference between knowing and admitting it. I couldn't bring myself to do the latter. Not now.

"You thought I killed Cam." He squeezed the plastic bottle hard enough it crunched. "And I guess Dani, too."

What was I supposed to say to that? It was true, but saying that would tear everything apart. The right words didn't exist for a situation like this. I couldn't kick him a meme with a shrugging six-year-old and be done with it, even if we did have Wi-Fi.

"You had blood on your face and your hands." I choked on the words.

"So did you when I found you and Aubrey with Cam, and I

didn't think you killed him." He didn't yell, but there was a rage boiling beneath his whisper.

"That was before." Before we'd all become suspects.

"So you standing over a body is different than me? I see."

Clearly he did not.

"No, I only mean it was before we knew the killer was in this house. My nerves are shot, Liam. I didn't know what to think. My brain short-circuited. I can only take so much blood and grief and broken friends before my mind goes to all these dark places." Tears tracked my cheeks and my chest burned with a desperate need to scream.

He stepped near me, close enough that I could feel the heat from his breath on my exposed skin. "But *me*?"

It was the pain poured over those two little words that broke me. My shoulders shook, and I couldn't get enough air. The first sob burst from high in my throat, the next from the center of my chest like my heart was squeezing itself into each breathy cry. My fingers folded into his shirt, gripping the material like everything could be fixed if I held it firmly enough. Liam stumbled forward and wrapped his arms around my back. I burrowed my chin against his chest. It was easier to breathe when I didn't have to see his stricken face.

Even against my ear, there was a wobble to his words. "I couldn't do something like that, Kylie. I *wouldn't*."

I'd snapped something in Liam. Something big. How did you repair the wounds that left someone shattered?

"I know," I said, and mostly meant it. I *wanted* to mean it. "Sorry. This whole thing has scrambled my brain."

My sobs eased in his steady embrace.

"I'd thought the worst thing that would happen this weekend was you ditching me." His laugh shook my chest, loosened the guilt gripping my lungs.

"Same." I curbed the sobbing.

He pulled back and looked down at me. His stormy eyes had softened. "We are bad at worst-case scenarios."

I wanted to bury myself against his chest and pretend there weren't two dead bodies in a bedroom one flight up. But that wasn't an option now. I'd let others plan this weekend. I'd let them handle the details for prom. I'd even asked Aubrey and Rory to consult on my dress. I was done allowing others to make decisions for me.

I wasn't going to end up like Dani, and Liam wasn't going to be taken from me. No one else would die in this house if I had anything to say about it.

I settled my hands on Liam's shoulders, hanging on to him while my limbs solidified. "I know you have faith in Noah's Boy Scout skills to get us through this . . . ," I started.

Liam flattened his lips into a firm line. But by this point, stern looks didn't have much of an effect.

"Don't make that face." I waited for him to relax before continuing. "He might be prepared for dealing with this storm, but that doesn't mean he knows what to do about our friends being killed."

Liam flinched. Was that too blunt? My heart picked up its pace again. I wished it would stop running suicide sprints while we were locked inside a freaking murder house.

"It's just that he doesn't know what to do here either, and ignoring what's happening isn't going to make things better. It never makes things better." My lower lip was quivering and I didn't know how to stop it, but my voice was steady and that had to be what mattered most.

"I don't want to pretend this isn't happening." He tilted his head back, peering into the darkness overhead. "Well, I *do,* but it isn't safe."

I squeezed his shoulders. "None of us want this."

"Someone does." He lowered his gaze back to mine, and his rueful tone was matched with a gemstone flare in his eyes. "That's what I don't get. How could one of our friends do this? Are we sure it's someone here?"

I couldn't carry that kind of hope now. It wouldn't help us. "How would someone have gotten inside? We can't go out because of the downed power lines. So some rando killer couldn't come in."

"Maybe they were already in the house. Hiding somewhere?" He had to know how ridiculous that sounded. The house was big, but not *that* big.

"What room haven't we looked in?"

"I found Cam in that closet."

I swallowed hard. "I'm not checking closets."

Liam's brows drew tight. "Why not? The tight spaces thing?"

Sweat slicked my back. "I don't do closets. I—" No matter how bad I felt about kind of calling him a killer, I couldn't give him this piece of me. Not yet. "Confined spaces just make me really uncomfortable, okay?"

"Of course." He replied so quickly, so earnestly, it almost made me wish I wasn't holding back. "I can poke my head in a few closets. No big."

Relief shouldn't have come so quickly, but I clung to it anyway. "Cool, but where else could they hide?"

The storm droned behind me, but Liam didn't have an answer.

"I don't want it to be someone we know either," I continued, "but it isn't safe to pretend it isn't."

"I know," he grumbled.

Did he, though? He'd skipped off with Noah alone. He'd ignored the agreement we'd all made. He'd left *me* in the living room asleep and unprotected. I let go of his shoulders. He stretched forward for me, and I stepped out of his reach.

"What? Kylie, I can barely see you in here. What's going on?" He stepped to the side, so the candlelight could warm our faces.

"You left me." Purple and black clouds warred outside the kitchen window. The storm was rallying.

"Are we going to rehash this already? I thought you—"

"I need to know if you're going to stick with me," I blurted. My chest vibrated with the sudden rush of honesty. "If we're going to get out of here, I need to know that you're going to have my back. But if you're going to leave me alone again, just say so now."

His thumb was gentle on my chin but directed me to face him fully. "I'm with you."

"Even if Noah suddenly thinks it's a great idea to go outside or sneak off to raid more closets?"

"I said you were right, and I meant it." His fingers skimmed my jawline. "We need a plan."

I nodded, pressing my cheek more firmly into his touch. "We had one."

"We did, but . . ." He hesitated.

"But?"

"Staying together isn't really a plan. It's a good idea, but we need to try to pinpoint who did this and protect ourselves from them."

I wanted to be safe, but what if we got this wrong? My chest deflated beneath the weight of the responsibility. "Where do we start?"

"We need to look at Vic." There was an unfamiliar harshness to his words, but his touch remained light.

"Vic? He's a jerk, but he stuck with Aubrey and me while we came to find you."

"Maybe he did that because he knew what you'd find."

"Then why didn't he stop you guys?"

Liam dropped his hand from my cheek. "I don't know. Maybe he didn't hear us go?"

That didn't seem to me like much of a reason to suspect him. "What makes you think he's someone to look at?"

"He's new, for one."

"So's Holli."

"She's not a creep, though."

"A creep? You guys wouldn't have let Noah invite a perv here, so what kind of creep?"

Liam opened his mouth but didn't say anything. My stomach hollowed out.

"What kind of creep, Liam?" I asked more firmly.

"Have you ever noticed he disappears at every party?"

"Not really. I mostly ignore him."

"I found him poking with the router box at every house—including mine—and he was on Noah's tablet every five seconds last weekend. He had a phone in his pocket. What did he need with Noah's tablet?"

"Maybe he was doing some jailbreak thing for Noah." As soon as the words left my mouth, I knew how wrong they were.

"For Noah?" Liam might as well have rolled his eyes.

Noah and Vic were in the same coding classes. The same electrical engineering groups. Noah didn't need help jailbreaking anything.

"Okay, so he's poking at networks when he's at other people's houses. Weird, but how does that flag him as a murderer? I mean, isn't that mostly him leaving everyone alone?"

"I don't know that it makes him a murderer, but it makes me think he has secrets."

Didn't we all? Spilling my past wasn't on my agenda. So far no one had called me on avoiding the small spaces. No one had noticed that I stayed close to the lanterns and candles. I could handle darkness, but they didn't need to know why it bit at the back of my mind. What if Vic's secret was mired in shame, too?

It didn't matter. If we were going to make it out of this house alive, we needed answers. We needed the truth. We needed to mine everyone's secrets and stop the killer before they took another life.

I nodded once, more to myself than to Liam. "So that's where we start. Let's talk to Vic."

# twenty-four

VIC DUG his heels into the tile in front of the fireplace, refusing to sit. "We are not doing this again."

"Someone in this house is behind all of this." I didn't mind the new, stern Liam.

A sudden clap of thunder made us all jump.

"Not the storm." Holli's addition earned her only glares.

Vic ignored her, though. "Yeah, I get that. You all need to quit looking at me like I'm capable of that kind of evil. Seriously?"

I didn't want to accuse, but facts were facts. "You were the last person to see Cam alive."

"Your boyfriend was the last person with Cam's blood on his hands, but apparently that's chill?"

I clenched my jaw, giving myself a few moments to think. Half the room had seen me scream at the sight of Liam smeared with someone else's blood. None of them had seen me question him among the shadows in the kitchen. How did I reply to this without looking like the asshole?

"Liam answered my questions," I said finally. "That's all I'm asking of anyone."

Vic's shoulders stiffened. "Who decided you get to ask all the questions, again? You have a notebook so suddenly you become the official inquisitor?"

"I didn't see you volunteer. Besides, she was the one willing to do it in a fair way," Liam said, leaning toward the center of the room.

Vic folded his arms into a barricade at his chest. "Yeah. Real damn fair."

Rory tilted her head to the right. "What's answering the questions going to hurt you? I mean, if you didn't do anything, just get it over with."

There was an edge of defeat to her words, and I didn't want to acknowledge the flickers of fear cutting across her visage. Maybe Rory had finally realized how bad this really was.

Vic saw it, too, and pounced. "If it isn't offensive to be accused of killing your friends, then you go first."

Before she could say anything, Liam interjected. "You can't pass this mic here. You have to go first."

"Why?" Vic frowned and started to pucker his lips, but winced against the split lip Hudson had given him.

Were we looking at the right person? What were the right questions here anyway?

"Because everyone is freaked out that you're fighting it." Holli's words were drenched with fatigue.

The room stilled, and the steady crash of rainfall against the house echoed in the living room. It wasn't Vic who spoke first, though.

Noah ambled across the room to stand shoulder to shoulder with Vic, their backs to the hearth like some macabre greeting card.

"Our plan has been to stick together. Doing that has kept us alive." Noah's chin rose with his voice. He might as well have been giving a speech in a Fourth of July blockbuster movie. "Pointing fingers doesn't help that."

"Pretending this is normal and that we shouldn't be scared doesn't help either," I said, surprised by the indignation brimming in my gut.

Noah dropped his head as if in prayer, and when he lifted it, his eyes were on me. They were full of false softness; he might as well have said, *"Oh, honey,"* and patted me on the head. "You think alienating Vic is going to help?"

"He's alienating himself. Everyone agreed to talk, to help figure out what had happened—"

Vic jumped in, "And I did that. I told you about Cam and the tequila he jacked from me."

"You can stop talking about his drinking anytime," Aubrey said from behind her knees. She was balled up at the end of the longer couch.

"It doesn't matter now," Hudson said softly from her side.

"It matters." Her voice was gravelly, like there was concrete churning in her throat. "He was working on it. Having everyone talk about it behind his back would have been the absolute worst."

It wasn't behind his back if he wasn't here anymore. I could tell that we were all thinking it, but no one said it aloud. No one wanted to be the person who threw Cam's death in Aubrey's face.

"Okay," Noah said slowly. "If Cam's secret is out, then we should honor that by holding nothing back."

Aubrey bristled.

Noah nodded to her. "We can answer each other's questions."

"Thanks," Liam said. His jaw was rigid.

"At least your messed-up, all-truth version of Truth or Dare will pass the time," Noah muttered under his breath.

"Whoa. Wait. I didn't agree to this." Vic edged away from his closest friend.

Noah clapped a hand on his back. "What else are you going to do? Answer the questions and move on."

It sounded so simple, so routine. Did Noah really think this was a game? Why wasn't he scared? Preparedness was one thing, but this "whatever" attitude was next level.

I must have been scowling, because Liam elbowed me. "You want to start?"

"Sure." No, I didn't. What I wanted was more than just the facts. I didn't need to know where he'd been sleeping when Dani crashed to the foyer. I wanted to know how he felt about me, about Liam, Noah, and the rest of us. I wanted to know if he saw himself as our friend. I needed to know if we mattered to him.

Getting answers had to be the path out, right?

"Why did you want to come to the Shore house with us?" I tried not to sound like I hadn't wanted him here. Truthfully, though, he was the only person whose motives I questioned for sharing the rental house with us.

"*That's* your question?" At least I'd surprised him.

I shrugged. "Seems as good a place to start as any."

He rolled his eyes but didn't abandon his post at the mantel.

"It's a fancy-ass house on the beach. Who wouldn't want to crash at a Shore house for the weekend?"

Hudson chuckled. I didn't.

"But why us?"

"He's our friend," Noah answered for Vic.

I sucked my lips to keep from correcting him.

Aubrey was still salty from the talk about Cam's drinking and obviously did not have the same concern. "No, he's *your* friend. I barely know him."

"Ouch." Vic clapped a hand to his heart.

"She's right, though. Why'd you want to hang with us?" Rory eased forward from her slouch against the back of the couch.

"Why'd she let me sleep in her room the other night if we aren't friends?" Vic replied.

"She didn't," I corrected. "You agreed to help watch over her, but she wasn't even awake at the time."

"I did a nice thing to help take care of someone I thought was my friend, and you're making it sound like I'm a jerk. I wasn't trying to climb in her bed. I was just keeping Noah company and making sure she wasn't alone."

"You're totally right." I had to shut down this line of questioning. He'd agreed to help, but also continuing to poke at why he'd done it wouldn't help us get to the truth of why he wanted to spend the weekend with *us*.

Vic gave a low grunt.

"He came to the house with us because I invited him." Noah's exasperation was palpable. "I thought my friends might want to become real friends with him. Didn't think you'd be like this."

Liam leaned against the back of the love seat. "I get that this sucks, but it's not like Vic just met us this weekend."

Was he saying Noah's argument was invalid, or was he defending Vic? Emotions were high, but these mood changes were going to give me whiplash.

"You do sneak off at every party." Holli's voice squeaked even as she said it. I could tell she didn't want to be part of the pile-on. I didn't like backing Vic into a proverbial corner either, but the constant threat of being murdered was wearing away my politeness. And, anyway, getting these answers was a type of kindness. Once we had them, we could get past the worst of this and finally move forward. Even Vic.

"Ehhhh." Hudson's exaggerated shrug was too casual for this room.

Aubrey pivoted, giving Hudson her full attention. "What? Now you don't care if we don't get answers from him? You were the one telling me we should toss him out the front door."

"We aren't throwing anyone out," I said with an authority I didn't actually have.

Vic's shoulders were hitched near his ears. His wild mop of hair dipped over his forehead, casting dark shadows under his eyes. His stocky body was angling for a fight, but his eyes kept skimming the front door as if fleeing were a real option. Could the kid who only wanted to run really have done this?

Regret roiled in my belly.

"He just sneaks off at parties to change the name of the Wi-Fi network," Hudson said.

"He's never changed my Wi-Fi." Liam spoke to Hudson, but his attention on Vic never wavered. What was going on with these two?

"Maybe you don't hate dubstep as much as I do." Hud almost laughed. "He just swaps my dad's serious 'Williams' Guest Access' to the name of some garbage song he likes."

"You should really put a password on that," Noah said, like we weren't debating Vic's capacity to kill our friends.

The muscles in Liam's forearms were corded; everyone else in the room had relaxed by a degree, but he and Vic were still visibly strained.

"Is that good enough for you? I didn't realize wanting to hang out with you guys was something only a murderer would do." Vic sneered.

Noah dropped into the overstuffed chair. "You're new, man. Admitting that isn't a crime."

"Then why aren't we asking her why she wanted to be here?" Vic pointed at Holli.

"She's my girlfriend," Rory said. The "you idiot" at the end of her sentence was silent.

"So? I'm friends with Noah and that didn't stop everyone from questioning how I could possibly want to spend the weekend at a Shore house without wanting to kill everyone here."

My stomach shifted, and I was glad our food options were limited. Vic really did toss that whole murder detail around a little too easily.

Holli gripped Rory's hand. "I'm friends with most of the people in this room. I have been since I moved here."

Noah raised a hand, like it mattered. "Devil's advocate?"

Nothing good ever came from anyone pulling that move. I opened my mouth to stop him, but the tiny burr of doubt that had buried itself in my chest wouldn't let me. If I could push

Vic, we could push Holli. Everyone had to be equal here or it was just a witch hunt. Asking questions wasn't about inflicting pain; it was about keeping us alive.

That realization didn't stop me from flinching when Noah asked, "Why don't you ever talk about yourself?"

Holli nibbled at her lower lip. If she'd been wearing her signature ruby-red lipstick, her front teeth would be practically bloody. "I talk about myself."

She hadn't bothered to even pretend that was truthful, and it was the opening Noah had waited for. "No, you talk about Rory."

She leaned against her girlfriend. "I'm proud of her."

"She talks about herself," Rory said sharply to Noah. "If you were a better listener, you'd know that. Maybe that's why Dani wouldn't date you."

"Don't you bring her into this." Hudson was on his feet, chest heaving, his eyes wide.

Rory followed him up from the couch as if she were truly going to go toe-to-toe with him. "Noah wants to talk about my girl, then he should have to talk about his secret with yours."

"Dani is dead," Hudson spat. "We don't talk about her."

"We don't talk about her because this is about Holli." Noah slouched deeper into the chair. "This is about Holli hiding who she is. Do we even know your girlfriend, Rory?"

"Whoa. I know Holli," I said. She was sweet and kind and had a way with acrylic paint that I most certainly didn't.

The patronizing look Noah wore only solidified my position. "She paints beautiful abstract pieces and these so-heady-they-hurt paintings. Her school in Florida had whole afternoons dedicated to art."

Not that I was jealous. I was almost done with high school. NYU would let me craft with clay far more often.

"Knowing she's from Florida isn't the same as knowing her." My head whipped toward Aubrey as she spoke. I hadn't expected her to join the pile-on, but twenty-four hours could change a person. Or so I was learning.

If she were here, Dani would have cracked a joke about how we couldn't ever truly know anyone and cut the tension. Instead, the air thinned and the tiny muscles between my ribs screamed for oxygen. I swallowed hard, like it would force my lungs to remember their role.

"Screw all of you." Rory sidled in front of Holli, even though no one was making any move to touch her girlfriend. "If you want to say you don't know her—which is a complete lie—then you can trust that I damn well do."

"New doesn't mean evil," Holli said gently. "Just because you grew up together doesn't instantly make you friends. It doesn't mean you'll stay friends."

I drew in a heavy breath. It was enough to draw Liam's attention to me, but not enough to wipe the scowl from his face. He stretched a hand toward me, but I shook off the attempt at comfort. Nothing about this should be easy.

Liam nodded slowly to himself, like he had come to some decision. He licked his lips and then said, "I don't think Holli could have taken on Cam."

Rory coughed against the back of her wrist. "That's your argument? Not that she's a good person or that you trust me or her, but that she's not strong enough to kill a man?"

Holli's manicured nails curled around Rory's hip. "Babe? Could you not argue that I killed anyone?"

Rory dropped back onto the couch next to her girlfriend. "Sorry."

"Not trying to offend anyone. All I'm saying is Cam wasn't exactly a little guy. Even if she did have the strength, how would she reach his neck?"

"He could have already been on the ground." Vic plucked at the hem of his shirt.

"It does not help your case to go all hypothetical like that," Noah said in a stage whisper.

Vic finally dropped his tough-guy stance. "Everyone has already made it clear that pretending we don't know anything isn't helpful." He gave Noah a meaningful look.

"What *do* you know?" I asked, too quickly.

The blood was in the water. Was Liam right about Vic? Was I wrong? Was it all about to go to hell at the speed of Kingda Ka at Six Flags?

No wonder I felt like I was going to puke.

# twenty-five

LIGHTNING FLASHED behind the cardboard-covered window, and the momentary brightness illuminated the sharp angles and wan figures of my friends. By the next breath, the shadows had reclaimed the hollows of our bodies.

Noah's lips flattened into a harsh slash across his face. It was the first time I'd seen him truly look grim. "What is it that you think I know?"

"I—I—I—" Vic stammered, cutting glances from me to Noah and back again. "I just meant there's no point in not being fully honest."

"I don't think that's what you meant." My placating tone didn't dampen the prodding.

"It's nothing." His body was practically vibrating with how *not* nothing it was.

"Then it won't hurt to tell us," Liam said.

"He just thinks he can make you leave him alone if he gives you something." Why was Noah sulking?

Vic looked at him like he had the same question. "You want to know why I came here this weekend?" Sourness dripped from Vic's words. "I came because he wanted me to, and Noah's my only friend. There. You guys happy? I'm weird and I make people uncomfortable and people don't stick around that long. Except for him. So when my only friend said that if I came here, you'd all become real friends to me, I believed him. But none of it mattered, did it?"

I hadn't much cared for Vic, but now all I wanted to do was give him a hug. I turned over every interaction with him in my mind and tried to see the real him. The lewd jokes were to keep a distance. His offering to watch over Aubrey was to avoid being alone. Coming with us to find Noah and Liam wasn't only about finding his lone friend; it was also about trying to build something real with us even with the world falling apart around us.

"Vic." Liam was shaking his head. "I said it was cool to invite you here. We wanted you to come."

The others nodded to varying degrees, whether out of remorse or because they'd changed their minds about him being a potential killer, I didn't know.

Vic brushed him off. "Yeah, whatever."

Even through my sudden rush of sympathy, I didn't forget what he'd said before. If I cared about him and everyone in this room—which I most emphatically did—not asking the hard questions wasn't an option.

"I still want to hear whatever it is that you know."

"Hmm?" I didn't buy his dazed response.

He might want to backpedal, but we were past that. I'd pull the truth from him like boardwalk taffy if I had to, if it meant I'd make it out of the prom house alive.

"You said you knew something. It sounded like it was about

Cam." I waited a half second and then added, "You say we're friends. If that's true, we need to know."

Emotions fluttered over his face as my words hit the mark. I tried not to squirm as I watched the melee of confusion, hurt, pain, regret, and acceptance. I didn't apologize or take it back, though. I was discovering I was more focused on doing what was right than what was nice.

I hoped Vic was, too.

He licked his lips, his tongue darting anxiously over his mouth. "Cam was already on the ground when someone stabbed him." It came out in such a gust that the candle flames should have swayed.

A riot of questions charged the room. "What?" "How do you know?" "Are you sure?"

It was Aubrey, though, who quieted everyone. "Did you kill him?"

"No." Vic was both emphatic and somber. "No, I didn't kill Cam."

"Then how do you know he was on the ground when he was stabbed?" I asked. "You told us earlier he stole your tequila and then you left to find Noah." I didn't have to consult the notebook lying open across my thighs to remember those facts.

"The window in Hudson and Dani's room. I was looking out of it . . ."

"What were you doing in my room?" Hudson bellowed, drawing himself up to his full intimidating height. "You being in my and Dani's room doesn't make me think you didn't kill her."

"Fucking A." Vic grabbed the water bottle from a nearby table; it crumpled in his hand. "I didn't kill anyone. I'm trying to tell you I *saw* Cam being murdered and all you can care about is that I was in your room? You can fuck right off, Hudson. Fuck. Right. Off."

Hudson tilted his chin until his neck popped with a resounding crack.

"That was our fault," Liam offered.

"*What* was your fault?" Panic kicked my voice to soprano.

Liam's reply came riptide fast and steady. "Hudson's bedroom. Not Cam. Geez. Their room had the best roof access."

"It was the shortest climb to get out near the pool," Noah added.

Right. I shook my head. How had I already forgotten the way this weekend had begun? My cute little bikini and Liam in those board shorts? That insane leap from the roof that could have cracked his skull but ended in laughter? Now the thought of teetering atop the rooftop shingles and diving in the pool sounded comparatively safe.

"You could have said that," Hudson grumbled.

"Fine," Vic said. "I was in Hudson's room trying to find Noah and Liam so we could dive into the pool. Happy?" He waited for a begrudging nod from Hudson before continuing. "I didn't find them, but I saw Cam."

"What did you see?" I prodded, hating how badly I wanted to know. I had literally scooted to the edge of my seat.

"I didn't know it was Cam," he said, like the clarification changed the story. "I saw two people out by the firepit, though."

"Why didn't you say anything?" We could have known sooner. Aubrey wouldn't have had to find her boyfriend like that. I wouldn't have seen him either. Dani might be alive. What if we'd known before we'd been blockaded in the house? Before the cops had showed?

"I didn't even know it was our people." He turned to Noah. "I was going to tell you that I'd seen people crashing our rental, but then the bigger guy was on the ground and the other one was on top of him."

"What did these guys look like?" Noah growled. We all seemed to press in, waiting for his answer. Now wasn't the time for Vic to hold back again.

Vic shrugged. "Visibility was garbage."

"It wasn't black outside back then," Liam said with rueful reluctance. The storm hadn't started in full force until after we'd found Cam.

"I don't know what to tell you. There were two shadowy dudes. One was taller than the other. It's not like I heard screams or anything. I didn't even know what had happened. I definitely didn't think the guy on the ground was *dead.*" Vic's defenses were stacking between us again.

Hudson scowled at Vic for a moment and then said, "Well, where were you two? What'd you see?"

He tilted his chin toward Liam and then Noah.

"Diving off the roof, I guess." I bristled at Noah's blasé attitude.

"Vic was looking for you guys on the roof. Did he find you?" I asked Liam to avoid snapping at Noah.

"They weren't on the roof yet," Vic supplied quickly.

"Where were they, then?" Rory asked, still angled in front of Holli like a bodyguard.

"We met him in Hudson's room. He had just gotten there before us," Noah said, all "no big deal."

"It really was the best access point," Liam added.

"And you didn't see anything out by the firepit?" I asked. I wasn't sure if I wanted him to say that he *had* seen something so we'd have answers or that he *hadn't* so I didn't have to field another lie from him.

"I didn't," he said. "All I could see was the pool." Liam lowered his head, like he'd wished he could have helped more, too.

My stomach plummeted. Whether he was lying or not, we were back where we'd started, with zero answers on our friends' killer.

# twenty-six

WHAT HAD we gotten for all this stress? Vic scrubbed his palms against his upper arms like he was freezing, and he wouldn't meet anyone's gaze. Not even Noah's, his lone confidant. Noah propped one ankle atop a knee and tapped a lighter against the heel of his boot. His face was awash with boredom, but a flickering twitch next to his left eye gave him away.

The rest of the room had fallen into quiet conversation, but I didn't know who I could turn to. Everyone in this room should be my *ally*. I was supposed to trust them all, but had that ever been true? If I could see them as potential killers, what did that say about our friendships?

I was supposed to be a good judge of character. I didn't just let people in the moment I met them. Except maybe Liam.

He clung to my hand now, a safety line, a promise, a plea. "What do we do?" He pitched the question low enough that it was only for me, but I didn't have an answer.

I shrugged and tried to eavesdrop on the rest of the room. It's not like I had any sense of decorum at this point.

"Why *don't* you ever talk about your family?" Rory was asking Holli. Frustration added fire to the question.

"I shouldn't have to" was all the petite punk rocker would say.

"It's not that you have to, but they aren't wrong. You don't tell people about yourself."

"I'm not my past or my parents or some story about how I skinned my knee at eight while trying to do a kick flip."

Rory mouthed the phrase "Kick flip?"

"Skateboard." Holli sighed. "The stories don't matter. Actions do."

"Sure. Actions are great. Hot. But why don't you share with me? I want to know you." Vic had gotten into Rory's head. If I didn't know better, I'd swear she was on the verge of tears.

"You know me." Holli kissed her girlfriend.

From the other couch, it sure looked like a cop-out move, but Rory kissed her back and their conversation became purely physical. Hudson and Aubrey pretended they couldn't see.

"How do I keep us safe?" Liam muttered.

This question might not have been meant for me, but I answered anyway. "Stay close to me. As long as we're together, we can watch out for each other."

He bumped his shoulder against mine. "True enough."

After a long pause, he added, "Shouldn't we ask more questions?"

"I think Vic has done his part for now." I doubted he was guilty at this point, and I didn't want to get him riled up again.

"'K, but what about Holli?"

"Didn't we already cover her?" It made sense that the same

concerns he'd had about Vic should apply to Holli, but I didn't like it. The realization was bitter.

"No." Liam's eyes narrowed, and I had to hope he wasn't imagining me as the killer. "She deflected and we let it pass because Vic had answers."

If I was okay with suggesting he was a murderer, I needed to treat her the same. Even if the act made my mouth go dry.

"Holli and everyone else," I agreed.

Liam relaxed against my side while I stiffened. I wasn't ready for another round of pointing fingers and prying open pasts.

"We're hitting the bathroom," Rory announced. Holli was already on her heels out of the living room.

"Now isn't the time for sink sex," Noah shouted after them.

"Or maybe now would be the best time for that," Vic replied with a suggestive eyebrow raise and a searching glance around the room. No takers.

# twenty-seven

HUDSON WAS the first to see the water. It made a grim sort of sense that it would be him. After all, he'd almost charged headlong into the electrified moat just past the porch, back when he'd been all anger. Back when his girlfriend had still been alive.

"Water" was all he said at first. The word hummed with impending doom.

Aubrey tossed her half-full bottle at him just as he had craned his neck toward the front door. The bottle thumped against his chest and dropped to his lap.

"We've got a problem." He stood slowly. The plastic bottle rolled past his knees and plunked to the floor.

"What's going on?" I asked. The foyer was too dark for me to see anything, except the mental image of Dani's body beneath that sheet.

Noah clamored over the rolled arm of the chair. "Seriously? No."

"What?" I asked again, louder.

Liam and Vic rushed forward toward Noah.

"What do we do?" Liam asked Noah.

The guys huddled near the door. No one was explaining the situation.

"Tell me what the hell is going on." I raised my voice loud enough that it would command attention.

Liam rushed back to my side. His eyes were wild, but his hand was steady on my waist. "Water's coming in under the door."

"Like it's flooding?" Aubrey pulled her feet up onto the couch.

I edged forward.

"Yes," I said, suddenly seeing what they'd reacted to. The room was dim, but liquid pooled at the base of the front door. It wasn't rushing in, but it creeped in the darkness. The foyer was filled with gray light, the storm tinging everything it touched. Its oozing spread almost reminded me of the blood that still saturated the entryway rug. But this was more fluid, more mobile, and more of an immediate threat.

"How do we stop it?" This time I looked to Noah, too. The Boy Scout had to know.

He floundered for a perfect answer. "I don't know. Sand-bags are what you use for flooding, but it's not like the pantry has a few fifty-pound bags of sand."

He scanned the room like Hudson or I had hidden piles of industrial supplies behind the sofa.

"There's sugar and flour in there, though," Aubrey offered.

"They'll melt in water," I said, like I didn't know she'd taken the same domestic life skills classes I had.

"And there's not enough of it," Noah added. "We could try putting towels at the doorways, but . . ."

Hudson had moved to the back of the room, like he couldn't get far enough away from the $H_2O$. "But it'll electrocute you."

The guys grumbled, but I just gnawed on my lower lip. "Maybe not?" I tried.

"You were the one who showed us what happens if you touch it," Vic said. I remembered the demonstration, but the electricity might not be distributed equally throughout the water, especially with how quickly the sea was stretching inland. The lines might have snapped farther up the path. Just because our power was out didn't mean all the lines had died. There were a lot of factors here about how deadly that water was to us. And no matter how zap-worthy it was, it could drown us if we didn't make a move soon.

"It might be less charged now." It was an oversimplification, but the water wasn't slowing and that meant time was finite.

"You want to touch it and see if you get shocked to death? Go to town." Vic was retreating now, too.

Liam's hand tightened at my hip. "It's too risky."

"He's right. We need to get to higher ground." Noah didn't wait for anyone's agreement. He marched past the blood-soaked rug and the brackish water edging ever closer to it, and took the first two steps upstairs.

"What about when the water rises higher?" Aubrey didn't lift her voice, but it sang through the room cleanly.

"We start planning a way to signal for help," I said.

Vic grinned. "Or those roof-climbing skills are going to come in handy."

He bounded after Noah up the stairs as if there hadn't been any tension between them. Was that a guy skill? Apparently he could drop grudges in milliseconds? I absentmindedly looked at Aubrey, who was coiled on her upholstered island.

Did we need to run? The water was steady but slow. It hadn't touched the carpet yet, and the wood floors had to mute an electrical charge. Probably. I should have paid more attention in my science classes, but I truly could never have predicted this scenario.

I turned away from the guys, from Aubrey, and started toward the kitchen. Liam caught my arm.

"Where are you going?" His grip wasn't firm, but the wildness in his eyes suggested it could have been.

"We need to know if the water is coming in everywhere." *I* needed to know.

I yanked my arm out of Liam's hold with more effort than needed. I stumbled forward.

"Let me check," he offered.

I followed him, because I needed to see it for myself. But the water wasn't yet creeping in from beneath the back door. That was something. I headed back to the living room before Liam could catch my eye. I didn't need to know if fresh hurt was building between us.

Hudson was trying to talk Aubrey off the couch. I ignored them and slipped behind the sofa to peek around the cardboard patches on the windows. The whitewashed planks of the wraparound porch had disappeared beneath sloshing grays and browns. The floodwater had swallowed the lawn, the three steps up to the porch, and now the floor itself.

The steel that'd held my spine straight earlier must have liquified. My chest tightened, my heart stilling beneath it. I might not need to worry about the killer in the house. Hurricane Winston might be the death of me.

Shallow waters had never scared me, but this would get deeper. It would stretch upward and grasp my legs. It'd pull me down into the darkness and hold me there. Even now, black edged into the corners of my vision. Readying to trap me.

"I'm not going anywhere." It was Aubrey's obstinacy that set me gasping air.

"We can't stay down here," I practically shouted. No one called me out on my fanatical tone or my uneven breaths, which were audible in the stagnant room.

"That's what I said," Hudson said in an exasperated voice.

"Are you going?" Aubrey was daring me. It was her go-to fear move. My go-to move was shutting down, and that wasn't an option.

I strode around the couch, keeping one eye on the flow eking into the house. "Yes."

"Thank God," Liam muttered. He wove his fingers with mine but didn't try to steer me to the stairs.

Hudson stretched his arms toward Aubrey. "I can carry you."

She let Hudson pick her up from the couch and cradle her against his chest. I'd never seen her like this; she was usually the type of girl who moved at her own pace. I squeezed Liam's hand. Would any of us be recognizable after this weekend?

Did it count as survival if we weren't the same people afterward?

I gritted my teeth and tiptoed around the spreading water that was starting to soak into the stately rug. I'd rather be cracked than killed, I decided. I could paint gold leaf over the broken bits of my pottery flops, but I couldn't mend what didn't exist.

We'd made it to the first landing when I realized with a start that our group had already been fractured.

Rory. Holli.

I said their names aloud, then dropped Liam's hand and pivoted. "They were in the bathroom. We have to go back."

It wasn't Liam who reached out to stop me, though. Noah stomped heavily onto the landing, and his forearm flashed in front of me, blocking my way. The spooky portrait glowered at him.

There were red and purple scrapes slashed up his arm. I shoved at him.

"That water isn't going to just go away," Noah said. "Not yet anyway. We need to get to higher ground." The hardness in his voice offered no negotiation.

Too bad I didn't care about his opinion. "Holli and Rory are still down there."

He swore under his breath but held his arm firmly against my ribs. Liam cupped my shoulders. His hands were warm, or maybe the chill of Noah's disregard had dropped my body temp.

"Noah." Liam only said his name, but there was both a plea and a warning in there.

Noah pulled his arm away from me and speared his fingers through his hair. Strands tousled down from his sloppy bun.

"It's not safe," he said mostly to himself.

"*You* said we needed to stay together," I retorted. I wished that flinging his mantra back at him gave me more satisfaction, but anxiety still had me in its grip.

He sucked his lips in until they disappeared. "We do."

"Great." I stepped forward.

Liam stopped me. "We go together, and fast. Straight to the bathroom, grab them, and then back upstairs."

He watched me for agreement before moving another muscle. At least he was getting better at this teamwork deal.

I nodded once, and then charged down the stairs before someone else could try to bar me.

They weren't in the bathroom, though. I rounded the corner to the short hallway and found Rory slumped against the door frame.

Holli was nowhere to be seen.

# twenty-eight

I RAN to Rory.

I dropped to the ground, ignoring the bite of hardwood against my knees, and grasped her shoulders. She didn't react. I tried shaking her, but she flopped like a rag doll.

"Rory?" I said her name louder and louder, but she didn't react. I skimmed my hands down her arms. No wounds. Her neck was unmarred. Her mouth was slack, but I found no blood on her face either. The bathroom door was cracked open, and the faint glow of a pillar candle warmed the space. It was the only flicker of life in the short corridor, besides me and Liam.

"What happened to her?" Liam asked from behind my shoulder. He hovered close enough I could almost feel the press of his body against my back.

"I don't know." Terror threatened to choke me, and I gritted my teeth against the wave of fire rushing from every pulse point.

Liam reached around me to touch Rory's neck. "She's breathing. She's passed out, but definitely alive."

*Alive.* Liam's lips cradled the word, like he knew how precious it was, like he'd been just as scared as I was that she was dead.

Rory was alive and I wasn't alone. I forced myself to push back the prickling adrenaline and focus.

I nodded once. "Holli."

Liam straightened. He launched himself forward, shoving the bathroom door open wide and shouting her name. The knob clacked hard against the tile on the wall behind.

He examined the room, the lantern he held in front of him gilding him in yellows and golds. Then he turned back toward me, and I knew. I bit the inside of my cheek until the pain centered me. It ached but didn't draw blood.

"Holli?" Everything seemed to be moving in slow motion.

"She's in here." Why did he sound so far away?

"A—" I couldn't say *alive*. It'd jinx it. "Is she okay?"

"She's alive, but . . ." At least he could say the A-word.

I steadied Rory against the wall and then stood to join Liam.

"But?" I asked, and then I saw her.

Holli was sprawled against the pedestal sink. Same parted lips, glazed eyes, and limp limbs as Rory. Only her forehead was cut open where it pressed against the porcelain. Red rivulets of blood ran away from the scene and down the column base.

"What happened to them?" Liam wasn't really asking me. Horror and confusion pulled his features tight. There was no simple answer.

I glanced back toward the end of the hallway. No one had come for us yet. "We can't leave them here."

A low sound of disgust punched from Liam's chest. "Of course not."

I couldn't apologize now. We didn't have time. The water in the foyer wasn't visible from here, but just because we didn't see it didn't make it any less of a threat. Time was running out. "How are we getting them upstairs?"

Liam dug his teeth into the corner of his mouth. "I can carry them, but what if I hurt them by moving them? Are you supposed to move unconscious people?"

"I don't know, but I think leaving them to drown outweighs the rules about moving them." My exasperation didn't really instill confidence. I tried again. "I'll run back and get someone else to help. The sooner we get them upstairs, the sooner we can figure out what's happening."

And help them. Because I needed them to be okay. To be safe. To not die.

Only nothing could be that simple. I took the small lantern from Liam and hurried back toward the stairwell. The water was no longer creeping into the house; it was pouring, filling, clawing. Two-thirds of the rug was wet. The bloody splotches left by Dani's body were now saturated with storm water.

The floor's subtle angle hadn't been noticeable before, but with the water rising, it was easy to see the tilt toward the front door. It's the only reason I was able to dart up the stairs without placing a bare foot into the creeping cold.

The landing was empty, aside from the judgmental scowl of the framed woman and the jovial trio of twentysomethings atop a schooner, grinning down at me from their picture frame. I'd expected the others to wait for us. At least one of them.

Noah was all about us staying together. So why wasn't he here right now offering a hand or a lighter or a rope or whatever else he kept in his Swiss Army pack?

No time for grumping. I stomped up the next set of stairs. Vic's chin atop the banister was the first thing I saw when I rounded the corner.

"Moving slow." He *tsk*ed me before realizing I was alone.

"I need help," I blurted.

Aubrey and Noah both rushed to the top of the stairs to meet me. Aubrey's eyes skimmed my body like a triage nurse, looking for something wrong, but Noah met my gaze head-on. He'd bundled his hair back up into a loose bun. Two long, light brown strands teased his right ear. That was the only light thing about Noah right now. His eyes were near black. It had to be the darkness of the second floor casting him so harshly. I lifted the lantern but only found thin lines furrowing his forehead.

"What do you need?" He looked behind me, and his breaths came faster. "Where's Liam?"

He quickly added, "And the girls?"

From below, Liam bellowed, "Where is everyone?"

I spun, using the lantern to illuminate the path. Liam appeared, lowering Holli to the floor on the first landing. He hadn't brought the candle with him. My stomach rolled.

Noah sprinted past me, his own camp light in hand. Vic sprang over the banister and tumbled down a couple steps before stopping next to Holli. "Who did this to her?"

His righteous anger only made me nod. That was the right feeling now. It was at least more useful than the fear bubbling in my belly.

"The water is coming in fast," I said before anyone else could jump in. Now wasn't the time for conversations. "Rory is still down there."

Liam turned toward the first floor again, but Noah stopped him. "Just tell me where she is."

"Outside the bathroom door. Right side." There was a formality to Liam's instructions. This wasn't a game and they weren't wearing headsets or commanding a fictional mission online. This was actual life or death. Our lives. Our deaths.

Noah nodded once and sprang into action.

Vic was gentle with Holli. He picked her up and cradled her head close to his, taking each step up the first flight of stairs with precision. Aubrey and I trailed behind him. He paused at the landing, and I came up next to him. "Where should she rest?"

I didn't think I was capable of smiling right now, but my chest warmed. He didn't ask where to put her or what to do with her. She wasn't a task. Maybe the guy really did just want to have real friends. If we survived, I'd just have to tell him to knock off the dick jokes.

"Can you carry her another flight?" I tried not to notice the way his knee was shaking, though Aubrey was looking pointedly at him.

He ignored it, too. "Of course."

"She can go in my room. I'm going to wait for—"

A string of expletives a mile long exploded from downstairs.

"Liam?" I shouted.

"I'm good," he replied immediately.

"I'm not," Noah grumbled. He tottered onto the landing

next to my boyfriend, still cursing beneath his breath. He slammed his heel against the floor repeatedly, Rory slumped at his feet. "You weren't lying about that damn water."

"You good?" Liam said like it was obvious his friend needed to suck it up. I shook my head; we didn't have time for this.

"Let's get our asses upstairs, okay?" Noah tossed Rory over his shoulder.

It was how firemen carried unconscious people. I'd seen it enough to know it was normal, but compared to the way Vic had held Holli, it seemed callous. He wrapped his other hand around her thigh and started up the steps again. I backed away from the top of the stairs to give them more room. It wasn't fair to be upset at him. I sure as hell hadn't attempted to pick her up, so could I really be saying much?

"We should go up another flight." Noah was winded, but his voice was clear.

"Vic's already halfway up there."

"We're not going to my room." Aubrey edged closer to me but didn't move to the stairs yet.

"No, mine." None of us could handle her room. It didn't matter that no one had died there. We'd found Cam's body for the second time in that bedroom. The blood was still on the floor, on the closet. Stepping in there would be nightmare fuel, not that I was going to say so aloud.

Liam's hand found my lower back and I jumped away from the touch.

"Sorry," he whispered.

I rolled my shoulders like it'd actually dispel my nerves. Wriggling my fingers didn't do a thing either. "It's fine. We should get upstairs."

He touched me again, and this time I didn't pull away from the warm, steady presence.

"Aub?" I prompted. She finally started up the stairs.

Her arms were wrapped around her body so tightly I was surprised she could breathe. They squeezed tighter with each step she took. Aubrey walked like this was a funeral march.

Maybe it was.

Maybe she could sense something I couldn't.

Whatever awaited us on the third floor, it had to be better than drowning or frying in the salty surge that was currently flooding the living room.

It had to.

Right?

# twenty-nine

PUDDLES OF wax with charred wicks held a mourning vigil on the nightstand. The flames were gone, and the bedroom I'd slept in was now steeped in gray. Light attempted to pierce the billowing clouds beyond the far window, but our only real illumination came from the lone camp lantern in Noah's hand.

The guys had placed Holli and Rory atop the duvet on my bed. They were still sleeping, if that's what we were calling this. I brushed the black wisps of Rory's hair back from her forehead.

"You don't have to check her pulse again." Noah leaned against the window, his lamp resting on the sill at his side like a stalwart guard dog.

"I just want them to be okay." My words were soft, but in the eerie stillness of the bedroom, nothing was secret any longer.

"We just have to wait this out." Liam kept returning to the same chorus. It didn't bolster my confidence this time any more than it had the last half dozen times he'd tried it.

"They're fine. Once their pills wear off, they'll apologize to you and we'll move on." Noah's sour tone struck me hard.

What right did he have to be bitter? He wasn't the one knocked out on the bed. He was alive and alert enough to be pouting. He poked at the steel pipe the homeowner had used to "lock" the window. Why the third-floor window needed a lock, I was beyond questioning.

"They wouldn't have taken anything *now*." I folded my arms across my chest, feeling defensive on their behalf. He didn't *know* they were drugged. I tilted my head to the right, trying to see Noah in a fresh light. He'd bounded up two flights of stairs with an unconscious person over his shoulder like it was nothing. Maybe it was time to poke at him.

Aubrey cut through my thoughts, keeping me from antagonizing anyone. "Wasn't I zonked like that, though?"

She slouched against the foot of the bed.

"Yeah, but that was before." I gestured in a circle like it could encompass everything we'd endured. "Someone had to do this to them."

"We have them now. How they got the pills isn't as important as the fact that they'll be okay. We just have to wait it out." I could practically see Aubrey clinging to the idea. As if waiting would get us out of here alive, get us answers, get us our friends back, get her boyfriend back.

I tugged my arms tighter around my torso, but it did little to calm my flip-flopping belly. Liam dropped a kiss on my shoulder and then walked to the far wall and slid down, slouching on the floor against the pale pink wallpaper.

"We'll keep them safe," Liam whispered to me.

"Knowing who did this would make us all safe," I said.

"It doesn't matter, Kylie." Hudson's mirthless laugh ping-ponged around the room from where he crouched in front of the dresser. We all frowned. "They aren't dead. That's our new barometer for what's normal. They aren't dead, and we can just ask them what happened when they wake up."

Hudson fastened his hands together and wrapped them around his knees, as if to stop them from twitching. Still he *sounded* confident. Did that mean his words carried truth, or was I just grabbing on to any granule of hope now?

My shaky nod must have still counted, because Hudson nodded back and then focused his attention on his joined hands. Everyone was listless. Aubrey stared into nothingness and Noah picked up the pipe and tossed it in his hand. Vic watched the pipe, but not his friend.

Talking would make this less awkward. If we talked, I might not have been able to hear the water sloshing beneath us and plinking against the outside of the house. The room wasn't shrinking, but my throat was. My airways instinctively knew the water was pressing against us from all sides now. My palms were already damp, and twin beads of sweat raced down between my shoulder blades.

I could be closed in here, shut in this house—this room—forever.

"Hey" was all Liam said, but it was enough to yank my gaze to his piercing eyes.

I gave him the best smile I could, which probably was a pure freak show. He patted the floor next to him. He sat midway between the bedroom door and the closet. Could I be that close to the tight, confining closet now? I took a tentative step forward. My knees were the kind of wobbly that induced nausea, but I didn't fall. His smile was more convincing than mine had been.

I'd just sit closer to the bedroom door. Yeah. It was open,

letting the room breathe. Letting me breathe. I took another step forward and heard the *washa-washa* of the water echoing up the stairwell. My ears buzzed with the sound. I edged backward, away from Liam.

Back was better than drowning from the inside. I took another retreating step. Yes, this was better. I could hear the muttering conversation between Noah and Vic on the viability of us rappelling from the room. If I weren't battling the pinpricks of fire in my chest, I would have shaken my head at them.

"Kylie." Liam cradled my name in his mouth. He posted one hand at his side, ready to prop himself up. "Come on."

"He's got you. You're good." Every word from Aubrey was delicate now, carefully selected and provided with forethought. She might have been trying to backtrack from the blowup earlier, but I'd take it. She'd seen me sweat-slicked and screaming before. She knew where this would go.

I swallowed down my nerves. "I'm good."

It was a hopeful lie, which was probably the best kind of lie. I stumbled my way to Liam's side and collapsed onto the floor. I was closer to the closet, but it was safer. Liam reached a hand out in the other direction and nudged the bedroom door closed. I bit the inside of my lip.

"What the hell, man?" Vic asked without the vitriol we'd come to expect.

"Barricade from the water downstairs," Liam said, as if it was logical, but no one bothered to call him on it.

"Whatever," Vic said. He turned back to Noah. "How long do these storms usually last?"

"He's not a meteorologist," I said without thinking.

"No, but he knows more about storm survival than the rest

of us." Vic presented this as a fact, but we were trusting that Noah wasn't simply making up his "tips" as he went. I shook off the salty thoughts. That was my anxiety talking. Noah hadn't done anything to make me think he didn't want everyone safe. He'd been focused on keeping us together.

"Well, at least we're all together again," I said. It should have pacified Noah.

His forehead twisted until his eyebrows were arced down in a vicious scowl. "This isn't how it was supposed to be."

No one argued with him. How could we? Our perfect prom weekend hadn't just gone sideways. This wasn't simply soaked chiffon or mud-coated stilettos. This was death and destruction instead of a weekend party. I'd meant to spend three days soaking up alone time with Liam. He radiated heat at my side now, but I'd considered him a potential murderer. I'd come here with nine friends—or at least eight and Vic—and would leave with so much less. No Cam. No Dani. Could the rest of us come back together after the accusations? The killer had ripped everything from us. An echo of loneliness vibrated among each person huddled in the room. We were together, but were we surviving?

Holli's pink curls were flattened against the pillowcase. Her chipped nail polish was no longer a sign of her punk rock sensibilities but instead just another broken part of her. Gnashing my teeth together didn't change our situation. The wood floor bit at my butt, but that couldn't distract me from the sight of the girls on the bed. It wouldn't let me ignore the fact I'd let the others point fingers at Holli. I'd had to consider her a suspect. Right? It didn't matter that I'd vouched for her. We were either all capable of doing this or none of us were. That sounded fair and just when I'd said it aloud, but in the stillness of my mind now? It was a weak excuse.

Had the killer gone after her because she'd had the spotlight on her? Had those questions marked her as the next victim, and they'd simply failed? Both Rory's and Holli's breathing were slow and steady. They were firmly alive, and other than the gash on Holli's forehead, neither *seemed* injured. How could I know until they woke?

"I meant it, you know." Liam bumped his shoulder against mine. "They really are going to be okay."

I scratched a nonexistent itch at my knee. "I know, it's just . . ."

"Scary?" he prompted earnestly.

I turned toward him. "Sure," I said, but that wasn't all. "It's just this could have been anyone." I waggled the word until it took on the shape of the threat.

Liam's eyes clouded. "Maybe."

"Maybe?" I asked a little too loudly. All the conscious people in the room turned to me, no longer avoiding direct eye contact.

"You're fine," Noah said like I was a petulant toddler. I'd babysat. I knew that tone.

"Nice of you to decide that for me," I snapped back.

He twirled that pipe from one hand to the other, giving the metal rod more attention than his friends. Classy. "It's a fact. You're not bleeding. You're awake. You're alive. You're fine."

"Dude. Back off." Liam's hands were already balled into fists.

Vic scooted a couple feet back from the window. "Whoa. Chill out, Noah."

"Our weekend wasn't supposed to go like this, but you're here together and can't even appreciate that," Noah griped.

"How are we supposed to appreciate this bullshit situation?" Hudson asked.

"We're still together. We can keep everything together, and it'll be safe." Noah's knuckles were turning white where he gripped the rod.

Hudson shook his head but refused to look at Noah. "You keep telling yourself that."

"It's true! You're all moping, but you're safe here with me." Noah's eyes flared wide and white for a moment.

"No," I said. Noah pretended he hadn't heard me, but I had the others' attention. I pressed my thumb against the bruise on the outside of my knee. The flash of physical pain became a sharp slap of encouragement.

I locked eyes with Noah. A muscle in his jaw ticked. Sweat spackled his forehead. *Appreciate the moment?* Get real.

"We aren't still together. Cam isn't here. Dani isn't here. Rory and Holli aren't even conscious. This isn't the weekend we were promised by a long shot, and pretending like we're all fine here together when Aubrey's boyfriend and Hudson's girlfriend are dead, when *someone* did *something* to the two girls lying on my bed, is the epitome of a dick move."

"I'm a dick because I want to keep the group together and alive?" Noah waved his hands like he was some street corner preacher promising the end of days. The pipe tapped the windowsill when he stretched his arms wide.

Vic's brows knitted together in consternation. "You're a dick for acting like our friends aren't dead."

"Since when were *they* your friends?" Noah shot back.

"Hell, Vic. I've got your back at every turn, and as soon as the others decide to be nice to you, I'm the ass? Maybe this is why you don't have any friends."

Vic flinched.

"Doesn't it worry you that whoever killed Dani and Cam could have poisoned them?" I pointed to Rory and Holli.

Noah's narrow nose was turning red. "It isn't that simple."

"How easy was it for you to forget about Dani?" Hudson straightened against the dresser. "She *just* died and you're talking about how we should be happy we're together? I thought you wanted her."

"I had her," Noah muttered to himself.

That got Hudson on his feet. "The fuck you just say?"

That pushed Noah to his, too. "Don't tell me how I feel. Dani was supposed to be mine."

"Women don't belong to you." The words were slurred. Rory struggled to prop herself up on the bed. Her elbow shook at her side.

Hudson's attention might have lingered on Noah, but Aubrey, Liam, and I bolted to the bed.

"Careful." I slipped a supportive hand behind Rory's back and helped her up against the headboard. Could she hear the rush of relief releasing inside my chest?

It took a couple attempts, but Rory finally asked, "Why does my head feel like it's stuffed with sludge?"

"We thought *you'd* be able to tell *us* what happened." There was an apology buried beneath Liam's answer.

"How'd I get up here? Where's Holl— Oh." Her eyes fell on Holli's form, still slumped beside her on the bed. In the pale light I thought I saw a tear glistening in Rory's eye.

Holli wasn't moving yet. If Rory was awake, shouldn't her girlfriend be, too?

"The guys carried both of you up here," Aubrey said as she gripped the footboard.

I didn't have time for subtlety. "Do you remember what happened to you and her?"

"What . . . happened?" She tested the phrase.

"We found you both knocked out," Liam offered.

"Passed out, really." No one had hit them that we could tell, and if I were in her situation, I'd want that fact to be clear.

"How'd her head get busted?" Rory stretched a hand toward Holli, squeezing her forearm.

"We think she hit it on the sink." I wet my lips and tried not to stare at the shoddy patchwork bandage I'd placed on Holli's forehead. "You were in the hallway."

Rory nodded slowly.

The guys had crowded around the other side of the bed. The whole scene far too deathbed confession for my taste. I sidled toward the headboard a half step. Just enough to get a little space. "What do you remember?"

"We were making out." She paused and shot a sharp stare at Vic, whose lips were already parted like he was ready to make some dirty joke. "If I could throw something at you, I would."

"Ignore him," Hudson said. "What else?"

"She got woozy. Not like light-headed from what we were doing or that mushy, I've-had-a-couple-beers feeling, but like wobbly."

"What about you?" Vic asked, all humor gone.

"I guess I did, too?" She rolled her shoulder like it'd loosen a memory.

"You don't remember anyone else in the bathroom with you?" Noah propped his fisted hands on the side of the bed and leaned forward. He loomed over Holli.

"Just us, a candle, and a bottle of water. Super-sexy."

"We need that bottle of water," I said automatically. They'd been drugged. It had to be that, and that bottle might prove it.

"Not exactly an option, babe," Liam said, and I thought of the water bottle still sitting on the sink in the downstairs bath. We'd had another opportunity to pinpoint our killer and had lost it.

Once I got out of this place, I'd leave the criminal investigations to professionals. Art school wouldn't require me to collect samples. I could look back and change my work. I could edit and find new colors that were better. Tracking down the person who had killed and drugged my friends didn't work like that, and maybe for all my planning, I simply wasn't helping anyone now.

Rory leaned toward the edge of the bed. "I'm going to be sick. Oh God, I'm going to hurl."

She cupped her hand to her mouth and swung her legs over the side. She staggered toward the door on trembling legs. Hudson met her halfway and looped a meaty arm around her back and under her arms. "Let's go," he told her.

"You"—Rory groaned—"you guys watch Holli."

I nodded, though she was already halfway through the door. Holli's chest rose and fell in that slow-and-steady pace of deep sleep. There wasn't a flutter of movement beneath her eyelids, but I knew she was in there. If Rory was mostly on her feet, then Holli would be, too. I needed her to be.

Noah and Vic retreated to the window, but Aubrey stayed close to Holli. Good, she needed someone to focus on.

"Hey." Liam pulled my attention. "She's going to be fine." His sun-kissed skin had dulled to Victorian painting pallor. He was on the edge of crumbling, and I didn't want to be the one that reduced him to rubble.

"I'm just ready to get away from here." There. That was honest, if not as hopeful as it'd sounded in my head.

Liam took my fingers in his and tugged me a few steps away from the bed. It wasn't like we had any chance of real privacy, but it felt good to be with him. If nothing else, at least this weekend had proven we could be a thing. A real thing. A long-term thing.

"Getting out of this house is probably everyone's top priority, but I get you." He nodded.

I let out a long breath. "After this weekend? I think I'm done with New Jersey. This"—I swirled my free hand in the air, trying to capture the awfulness that had turned these badass digs into horror-movie fuel—"has ruined it for me."

His shoulders slumped, but those full lips quirked up. "I get that."

The cool gray sky beyond the window was streaked with charcoal. "If I never see the Shore again, it'll be too soon."

# thirty

I LEANED against Liam. "Doesn't all this make you think going to a far-off college in the fall might be worth it?"

His smile was half-hearted. "My mom said the same thing."

"I like you close, but getting out of Jersey might be . . . better." I sighed. He could leave, too. Maybe he should. "Could you still accept at California State? Or at least come up to NYC with me?"

He tucked my hair behind my ear. "I think the tunnel is the most long-distance you want to deal with."

"If you hate it here so much, then you might as well break up with this guy now," Noah said, pushing off the windowsill and making it groan.

Seriously? I didn't even know he was listening to our conversation.

Aubrey snickered from her perch at the edge of the bed. "Jealous much?"

Noah ignored her and advanced on me. He was already more than halfway across the room. How was he moving so quickly? Why did he care so much?

When he reached me, his treacle breath poured over my face. I edged backward. My shoulder blades knocked into a door. *No.* I tried to edge to the right, away from the closet at my back, but Noah planted a heavy boot in my path. "You aren't supposed to leave home, and he isn't going with you."

"You need to quit talking for me." Liam's face was shrouded in shadows, but his snarl was undeniable.

Noah snapped his gaze to Liam but didn't budge in front of me. "You were thinking about moving to California and didn't tell me?"

Liam's voice was steady. "I don't have to run everything past you, man."

"She did this," Noah muttered.

"The only person *doing* anything is you," Liam said. "You're creeping the hell out of everyone. Just back off."

Noah's words came fast, like a nervous soliloquy. "Then help me out. You need to choose what you want most."

What I wanted was for him to back off, but the doorknob was biting into my flesh at the base of my spine.

"Give her space or she's going to lose it." Aubrey's voice was distant and weak.

"She wants to leave." Noah bumped his chest against mine. It wasn't a hard hit, but air rushed from my lungs and I couldn't refill them fast enough. He pretended he didn't notice. "She wants to forget about her friends and doesn't even care if that means they're in danger. How much could she even care about you or Liam?"

It'd been more than a decade since I'd been put in a closet. More than ten years since my bio dad had shoved me in the dark space and pinned a chair beneath the knob to keep it shut. No one here was going to put me behind that door. No one here was going to shove me into a cell and leave me to starve, leave me to cry until I ran out of tears. No one in my life did that anymore. Mom had kicked him out. The courts had kept him away. My stepdad—my real dad—still removed the hinge pins on closet doors for me in hotel rooms so they couldn't be closed. I knew this. My brain said I wasn't the small, helpless girl any longer, but my heart didn't care.

A hand gripped Noah's shoulder and yanked him backward. He wheeled away from me for a moment. Was it Liam? My vision was peppered with black.

I was mainlining adrenaline. It burned down my arms and lit the insides of my ears until I was swimming in the drone.

Noah was screaming at me, but I couldn't understand the words. He pushed against me again. I slid down the wall until my butt hit the floor. He curled over me, a looming tower of fiery anger.

The guy who had stayed cool in every emergency—our goddamned Boy Scout—was losing it on me. He was pushing me into this panic-driven personal hell, and he was doing it on purpose. *He knew my secret. He did this. All of it.* The thought zapped the soles of my feet. I tried to scramble back up, but he was so close.

Liam's wiry legs came into view, and then Noah was wheeling backward.

I needed to rally, to get on my feet, but my knees refused to cooperate. I wobbled and fell back to the floor. The rush of static was still in my ears.

Liam's arm arced wide, and he landed a haymaker at the edge of Noah's jaw. The other guy stumbled backward, but he recovered quickly.

"You. Don't. Need. Her." Noah's huffing breaths were coming faster and faster.

"You don't get to decide that, and you sure as hell don't get to hurt her." Liam shuffled his feet, fists up.

Vic had rushed to the edge of the fight. His arms pushed in and out like he was waiting to enter a professional double-Dutch contest. "You don't want to fight each other," Vic managed weakly. It was dismissed by both guys.

"I'm *helping* you. We're a team." A tendon in Noah's neck strained, sharp enough to cast a relief in the flickering light.

"You're not thinking about me. Tell me, what are you really doing?" Liam shoved logic into every syllable. Did he really think now was the time for reasoning?

It wasn't, and Noah proved it. He adjusted his right hand to hold the metal pipe lower, and then swung hard and fast. It collided with Liam's shin with a sickening *crack*.

Aubrey shrieked and pulled her feet up onto the bed.

Liam toppled to the ground, his leg cradled before him. I couldn't see the wound, but the tight pull of his lips and the tears tracking down his cheeks said it wasn't good. Why couldn't I get up? I needed to stop this, needed to rush to my boyfriend, needed to protect everyone in the room. I'd known Noah for years, but as he loomed over Liam, with a feral mane of hair and predatory eyes, I realized I hadn't known him at all.

After hearing that Liam had considered moving away for college, Noah had morphed into someone malevolent. Or had he always been this way? He'd loomed over me as if I were an enemy and not the girl he'd known for years. The gentle, reliable guy had drilled a pipe into his supposed best friend's leg. He was none of those things. We'd been placing trust in him— not just this weekend, but for years—and he was capable of this.

Capable of killing Cam. He had the muscle, he'd proven he could carry a person up the stairs easily, and he wasn't afraid to take a swing.

Capable of murdering Dani. He'd seen her as a possession. The girlfriend that should have been his. Only she wasn't, and instead of accepting that, he'd let the rage I now saw filling his eyes take over then, too. For Noah, killing Dani had been a better choice than losing her.

A guy who could throw the girl he loved down the stairs for not meeting his expectations was completely capable of stealing everyone in this room from this world. We were in even more danger than I'd realized.

I needed to stand, needed to *take* a stand before he took everyone from me, but my heart still pounded in my ears and liquid heat fused my joints.

Vic made his move, darting in to try to grab the pipe. Noah was quicker. He swiped the pipe wide and out of Vic's reach. His other hand stretched toward his "friend" and grasped him by the neck.

"You shouldn't have done that," Noah said, seething.

Noah rushed toward the window and shoved Vic forward like a battering ram against the glass. His skull thunked against the pane. Vic staggered, hands held high like he could stop another blow. Noah dropped the pipe, its clang barely registering, but he didn't let go of Vic. Dark liquid was pouring down Vic's forehead and over his bewildered face. Noah adjusted his grip, now holding Vic by the neck with two hands, and throttled him into the window again.

The snap of the glass made me cover my ears. Looking over my shoulder only proved no help was coming. Liam was sprawled on the floor, pinning the door shut. Aubrey hadn't run to him; she still cradled her knees to her chest on the bed. It was for the best. I'd seen what he did to his best friends.

"That window open enough for you, Kylie? Little air to clear your head?" Was Noah really taunting me right now?

My anger was incandescent. It boiled away the panic that had imprisoned my joints. I rocked forward to my feet and started forward, grinding my teeth against the persistent, roaring buzz in my eardrums.

"Ah-ah." Noah wagged a finger at me and pinned Vic's chest against the broken glass with a heavy forearm. Vic's head dangled out the window, and rain poured in through the hole in the pane. Vic screamed.

# thirty-one

THE STORM splattered the oak floor next to the tipped-over lantern, light reflecting in the water that pooled beneath it.

This was the picturesque bedroom where I'd kissed Liam. More than kissed. This was supposed to be my weekend retreat. My sanctuary.

My boyfriend was bleeding to my right. Liam tried to stand. He collapsed halfway with the bellow of a wounded boar. Hudson and Rory still hadn't returned. Aubrey was rocking like a tweaker, which didn't bode well for anyone. Holli was still unconscious on the rumpled bed.

There weren't other options now. Running wouldn't work. Our phone signals were still toast. Vic's body was slackening against both Noah's hold and the jagged framed glass pressed against his torso.

"You want to leave so badly? Go." Noah's sneer might have been directed at me or Liam or Vic. He'd been ranting beneath his breath and it was hard to tell who held his attention, but it was clear he wasn't pretending to protect anyone now.

I took another step toward him, but his eyes immediately

cut to me. He was haloed by the storm beyond the house, and his black pupils dared me to move.

"*Cam* wanted to bail, and look at where that got him," Noah growled. "Even after that, I was the only one who cared about bringing him back to us. You all left him out there. You were so busy with bandaging your friends and kissing *my* best friend. I was the only one who would bring Cam back to be with his friends."

I stilled. Noah had carried Cam upstairs. He'd been less than twenty feet from Liam and me when we were in the upstairs bathroom, and we'd been so focused on our pain, our needs, that we hadn't seen him.

I wasn't going to fail another person. I had to distract him, had to try to save Vic. "Keeping us together in this house isn't going to stop us from leaving for college."

"*You* can leave." He closed his eyes for a half moment, and his breath shuddered. "We don't need you. So quick to judge, to point a finger at your friends. So much for loyalty."

Was he completely unhinged?

He flicked out his tongue to lick his lips, the move both reptilian and unnerving.

"Liam's still going to Rutgers. He's still going to visit me at NYU." These were facts. Or I had to believe they were. Now wasn't the time to second-guess if we would be getting out of this house alive. "You don't get to stash us at your side just because you couldn't pass English Lit."

Even through the pounding rain against the house, I wouldn't have missed his sharp inhalation. "That doesn't have anything to do with anything."

I wasn't supposed to know. None of us were, but Liam had let it slip two weeks ago. I pressed onward.

"Oh, really?" Did Noah think his friends were toys he refused to share with the neighbors? "You're not graduating with us. You aren't part of our group. You won't go with us to college. You're *stuck here*, and we aren't."

With each sentence, I edged another step forward. The steel pipe was only a couple feet away. I could lunge for it, but I wasn't certain I was fast enough. Noah was addled, but he was still lithe and quick. And if he'd managed to take down Cam, he was stronger than I would have guessed.

Noah readjusted his grip on Vic, who merely whimpered.

"You killed our friends." I said it plainly, because it was a fact.

Noah only lifted his chin at me.

I tried again. "You stabbed your friend in the neck with a broken bottle. Tell me how that's an act of friendship."

He shoved Vic hard against the sill. I flinched. "He wasn't a friend. He was supposed to spend the weekend with us, and the first chance he got, he stole Vic's booze and went off alone to get drunk and ignore everyone else. Aubrey had cried over it a couple weeks ago, and he didn't care. He didn't want to come back, didn't want to do what was best for everyone. He told me he didn't care about any of us."

In my bones, I knew Cam had cared about Aubrey, but I could believe that his drunk ass had said something like that to make Noah leave him alone. It would have been just that, drunken talk. "And that was reason to kill him?"

Noah took one hand off Vic's neck. "It wasn't supposed to

be like that. I rented this house so everyone could understand how important our friendships are. So we could be away from everyone else celebrating deserting their homes. You can't just bail on your friends because society says you should move out. My plan was perfect and you kept ruining it. I killed the Wi-Fi so we could have a badass party without live-streaming it for people who didn't deserve to be here, and you guys all call your parents? I hadn't counted on the storm taking out the power, but that was an opportunity to fix everything. I didn't want anyone to die. This wasn't the plan."

Was that regret shaking him? Could I get him to release Vic? Would we be able to make it out of here alive—all of us? The potential for success squeezed against my vocal cords. "And what about Dani?"

He dropped his hold on Vic and turned on me, glowering. "That was an accident. She wouldn't even talk to me, much less kiss me anymore."

He might as well have underscored the declaration in a bold Sharpie. He believed his own hype.

"You loved her." It was the truth, but my voice still ticked up at the end, wanting the confirmation.

"She didn't want to leave him. Claimed she loved Hudson, not me. But I knew she was lying. You don't share a bed with someone for months, tell them your fears, and then just stop feeling something for them. I told her that, you know, and she just said she was moving out this summer." His eyes widened and his fingers fluttered at his sides. "She didn't mean to hit me . . ."

Whatever he was remembering, it hurt.

Good. Pain was a distraction.

Vic stumbled back from the window. His chest was drenched in blood where the broken glass had sliced into him. Noah's attention snapped back to him.

It was my moment. I wasn't usually the kind of person who took action without a sketch, but there wasn't time to draw trace lines. Noah was going to kill Vic, and who knew who else.

I didn't have time for first, much less second, thoughts. I tucked my chin to my chest and barreled forward, slamming my shoulder hard against Noah's sternum. Bone hit bone, and the impact reverberated up into my neck, knocking my jaw hard enough that I cut open the inside of my cheek. Blood pooled in my mouth. Noah's feet slipped in the water at the base of the window, and the backs of his thighs hit the windowsill. Momentum carried him backward, and his torso slammed through the window.

He screamed, high and sharp.

I wrapped my arms around his legs, trying to hold him inside the house. The fabric slid against my arms, burning my skin. I gripped tighter.

"Hold on," I tried.

I was not a killer.

Not until Noah's feet slipped past my hands, and he crashed into the floodwater three stories below.

# thirty-two

"YOU'RE NOT a murderer," Liam said for the tenth time. His tone had grown more emphatic, but his fingers skimmed my back in light circles.

Arguing wouldn't change anything. Everyone had seen Noah's body beyond the window by now. The murky water hadn't electrocuted him, but his body was splayed at sharp angles where he floated. His chin grazed the outside of his shoulder, an arm tucked behind his torso, his legs folded at the shins. He'd been crumpled by the fall before bobbing back up. The one I'd caused.

"You had to do it," Vic muttered from beside me. He was propped up against the headboard of the bed, next to a newly conscious Holli.

"She didn't do anything," Liam snapped.

But I had. "If I hadn't charged him like that . . ."

Vic took two rattling breaths. His wheezing was getting louder. "It could have been me who went out the window."

I rested a hand on his ankle. "You're going to be okay."

"This asshole storm." Rory was working a hole into the floor pacing near the door. "We need out of here."

Hudson hadn't sat down since returning to the bedroom either. "The water isn't going to kill us anymore. I mean, with the power lines."

He was partially right. "They might have finally killed those lines, but we're going to have to test the water's electric current with something other than our fingers."

"We need to just call nine-one-one." Aubrey hadn't put a toe on the floor since the fight, much less said a word.

"The signal's still out." Fatigue marked Holli's every move.

Rory had found her bottle of anti-anxiety medicine in the upstairs bathroom. It had been emptied. It was a miracle that both Rory and her girlfriend were alive, much less awake.

"We could try it again," I said, taking another deep breath.

I wasn't the person who was supposed to slam headlong into danger. Taking out the person who had murdered and drugged my friends wasn't me.

Or at least, it hadn't been until this weekend.

Seeing your friends' dead bodies, watching your boyfriend lose a battle with a pipe, and discovering a person you'd known for most of your life was the one who had caused it all? That changed a person, and I couldn't be the only one finding their skin didn't quite fit the same any longer.

"Do we have any phones with a charge up here?" Mine was probably floating in the first-floor kitchen.

Holli's and Vic's phones were still charged and accessible. We grabbed them both. Wi-Fi was still down, of course, but when Hudson leaned out the shattered window—all of us holding our breaths—he was confident he had a signal. The emergency operator didn't doubt us this time. They had a boat in the area, and she radioed the first responders on it—firemen and policemen—to reroute in our direction.

The houses along the shore were supposed to evacuate, but we weren't the only ones who didn't get the memo. We were, however, the only house on the street that lost lives during Hurricane Winston. As we'd suspected, the storm had been officially upgraded while we'd been on Internet blackout.

Our rescue should have been long and complicated, but the team was efficient. They asked about Noah's corpse at the edge of the house. We had to pass him when we left, and if I'd eaten anything, I would have lost it then. Instead my throat merely burned. Aubrey took my hand and squeezed hard while we floated away from the prom house.

Liam slipped an arm around my shoulders and pressed a kiss to the top of my head.

Against my ear he whispered, "I get that you don't want to hear it, but you saved us. If he could do that to Cam, to Dani?" He paused and swallowed hard enough his chest shook against my arm. "He would have done it to me. Thank you for saving me. No matter what you feel now, you're our hero, and I'm not going to let you forget it."

And he didn't. Liam showed up on crutches at my house the morning after we were rescued from the prom house, and returned every morning thereafter.

Which was good, because my mom was not keen on letting

me out of her line of sight after the news broke about what had happened at our no-big-deal, nothing-is-going-to-happen Jersey Shore rental house. Dani's mom was at our kitchen table at least once a week sobbing with my mom, which did not help the situation.

Liam helped. He didn't care if I talked about the nightmares, didn't make me expound on my feelings. He brought me sketchbooks and new types of clay. He studied each piece I made for at least ten minutes before opening his mouth. Sometimes he'd only nod at the pottery or sculpture, and I'd have to listen closely for the hitch in his breathing.

Rory had brought fresh bagels to my house that first post-hurricane morning, and she'd hugged me for a solid minute. You help save someone's significant other and you're back in the golden circle. I wished I'd been able to do the same for Aubrey.

While Rory—with Holli glued to her side 90 percent of the time—visited me nearly every day, it had taken Aubrey almost three weeks before she started speaking to me again. It wasn't that she blamed me, but Cam's death left a deep scar on her heart. It was hard for her to look at me and not see him. Understanding didn't make it hurt less, but as the summer progressed, we'd continue to try. I hadn't heard her laugh since the night we rented the house on the Shore.

Liam had taken me to see Vic in the hospital. He hadn't lost his sense of humor in the horror of our prom weekend, and while I still didn't laugh at his jokes, I was glad more than his body could recover from what Noah had done.

I didn't go to Noah's funeral. Vic went, claiming it was for closure. Liam went, too, because he'd needed it. He said

Hudson had been there, too. Hudson had gotten into a West Coast school, and he flew to California right after the funeral. He said it was for summer training, but none of us blamed him for wanting to get away.

We were all focused on what came next. It was better to think about the future now. Rory and Holli helped me pick out all my dorm essentials. Aubrey let me craft a vase for her dorm, and even smiled at the thought of the bright flowers she could keep at her bedside.

Taking it one day at a time was working for me. Keeping Liam at my side helped. He understood me, and when I moved into the dorm at NYU in the fall, I knew he'd take the train in on his free nights. I'd skip out for the weekends. I'd make more art that told the story. The real story. Something more honest than the tales beneath splashy, sordid headlines about our night of horror in the prom house.

Me and my friends got out of that house, and after this summer we'd prove we were going to do more than just survive. We were *alive*. And no one could take that away from us.

# acknowledgments

A huge thank-you to my extraordinary agent, Naomi Davis, for fast reads, insightful feedback, and being the kind of person who has a "favorite murder" in my books. *Prom House* wouldn't have happened without you.

Thanks to my editor, Wendy Loggia, for the chance to write such a fun book (murder and kissing are fun!) and for making deadlines work for a pregnant lady. Bonus points for Jersey insights.

While I could write a great list of amazing writer women who help make the process of creating stories far less solitary, I'll keep it short. Big thanks to Melissa Marr for "you know what you need" brainstorming sessions over whiskey and wine, to Megan Frampton not only for giving great advice but also for reading a second time when I was worried about pregnancy brain, and to Cathlin Shahriary for both CP moves and coffee friend dates (remember coffee friend dates?).

Finally, I wrote this book while pregnant with my first child, and you'll find *Prom House* has everyone thinking about change. The ways we approach it and what it means to do the hard things and the scary things to get to the even-better things. (Note: You can also just read it for the murder and the kissing. No judgment!) Becoming a mom is a huge change, and the best one I've ever made. So thank you to my sweet son for being with me for the first of many books—and the first of many big adventures.

## 1.

**THIS IS THE STORY** of a messed-up girl and how her family paid people to send her into the wilderness with a bunch of other messed-up kids in hopes it would somehow make them less messed up.

This is a real thing that happens.

It might even be an eventuality your parents have considered for *you*.

But this is the story of what happens when things

go

wrong.

# 2.

MEET DAWN. Dawn is the aforementioned messed-up girl. She'll be the protagonist and de facto audience surrogate for this little misadventure.

Dawn is seventeen years old and mostly normal. She lives in Sacramento with a drug dealer named Julian, who is roughly twice her age.

This is a continued point of contention between Dawn and her mother, Wendy. Wendy would prefer that Dawn *not* live with a drug dealer. She'd prefer that Dawn, you know, go to school and not just get high all the time and sneak into clubs.

She'd prefer that Dawn be at home, where Wendy and Dawn's younger brother, Bryce, live with Dawn's stepdad, Cam.

Dawn loves her brother.

She mostly loves her mom.

Dawn does not love Cam. Dawn resents Cam and hates that her mother fell in love with him. Her father's only been gone for two years, and it's too soon to be talking replacements.

Dawn can't stand to be near Cam. It makes her feel like she's betraying her dad. It drives her insane that nobody else sees it that way. That her mother could move on so quickly.

That's why she's staying with Julian.

And that's why she spends her days mostly wasted.

# 3.

**THE CAM/WENDY/DAWN THING** has been an on-going saga. You don't need to know the gory details, but suffice it to say, it's been a lot of screaming and hurt feelings.

It's been a lot of self-medicating and not going to class.

It's been a lot of *Julian*.

Cam and Wendy have been trying to get Dawn to come home. Go to school. Be high less. See less Julian. Be more normal.

Cam and Wendy have failed miserably so far.

But Cam and Wendy have one more bullet to fire.

It's their last resort.

And it's going to *royally* fuck up Dawn's day.

# 4.

WHAT IT IS, is a straight-up kidnapping.

Cam and Wendy show up at Julian's place at sunset. Dawn and Julian are on Julian's couch, watching cartoons but not really, when Cam knocks on the door. Dawn is too high to get off the couch; she lets Julian answer, hears the door open, hears voices:

Julian, someone else, Julian again.

Then Julian's back, scratching his head and not looking at Dawn.

"It's your stepdad," Julian says. "He says if you don't go talk to him, he's calling the cops."

From the way Cam's face twitches when he sees her, Dawn knows she must look like shit. She hasn't showered since whenever, her hair's a disaster, she's wearing one of Julian's Lords of Gastown T-shirts like a dress.

"What do you want?" she asks her stepdad. Looks past him and sees Wendy standing by the minivan, arms folded across her chest, looking anywhere but at the house.

(Dawn briefly wonders where Bryce is, then decides she's

glad he isn't here. She doesn't love the thought of her little brother seeing her like this.)

Cam sets his jaw like he's been rehearsing this moment. He probably has.

(He's probably not a bad guy, Cam. I mean, it's not *his* fault that Dawn's dad is dead. Cam's an accountant, and mostly harmless, and Dawn might actually like him if he were, you know, her *teacher* or something and not someone who acted like he was entitled to any authority over her whatsoever.)

"I need you to come with us, Dawn," Cam says. "It's time to go."

Dawn rolls her eyes, like she always does when Cam starts down this road. "I'm not going anywhere with you, Cam," she tells him. "And you can't make me."

Cam stares at her. Mouth opening and closing like whatever he rehearsed, it didn't get this far.

Then Julian shows up behind Dawn. "I think you should go," he tells her.

Dawn spins, like *WTF?* Julian shrugs. Cam's looking at Julian like he wants to punch him, but he won't—

(Julian's twice his size).

Cam just nods instead, like *Listen to the man.* "Nobody wants the police involved, Dawn," he says.

Cam has a point. Julian knows this.

Dawn knows it, too.

If the police show up, they'll find Julian's stash of pills. They'll find Julian, and they'll find Dawn.

Julian doesn't want any part of this, obviously.

So Julian's turned traitor.

Julian's practically shoving Dawn out the front door.

*Go with your parents, Dawn.*

*GTFO.*

So Dawn doesn't put up too much of a fuss. This has happened before. She's thinking Cam and Wendy will pile her into that minivan and just take her home, like they always do.

She's thinking this is just another bullshit power move by Cam to prove he's cut out to be her father, and she'll endure it for a couple of days on the absolute outside and then she'll sneak off again and do what she wants.

And this time she'll make sure Cam and Wendy can't find her.

This is what Dawn is thinking.

It's what she's expecting.

But Dawn is wrong.


Cam takes her to the airport.

*5.*

"THERE'S NO FUCKING WAY this is legal."

In the airplane seat beside Dawn, Wendy says nothing. She hasn't said much the whole plane ride, won't even answer Dawn's questions.

(Like, why are we on a plane?)

(Why isn't Cam coming?)

(Why did you pack me a bag?)

She's trying so hard to look tough, Dawn can tell. Play the authority figure, the mean mom, but Wendy isn't cut out for that role. She's too *nice*.

But she's trying to be tough, and it's clearly taking work, and watching her, it kind of breaks Dawn's heart a little bit.

(Like, whatever is happening, *you* made her do this.)

(*You* made her this way.)

Dawn would never admit it, but maybe that's why she isn't putting up more of a fuss. Maybe that's why she didn't go batshit and scream *kidnapping* when Cam dropped them off at the airport. Because for whatever reason, she didn't.

She put on the shorts Wendy fished out of her overnight

bag, watched Cam hug Wendy goodbye and drive off, and then she followed her mom into the airport and onto the plane and stared out the window and waited to land.

And now they're at the Seattle airport, and it's nighttime and there's a guy standing at the baggage carousel holding a sign with Wendy's name on it. He's around forty, tanned, wearing a blue fleece jacket with the words OUT OF THE WILD on it.

He shakes Wendy's hand.

He doesn't shake Dawn's.

"Come on," he says. "I'm parked in the lot."

# 6.

**THE FLEECE GUY'S NAME IS STEVE.** He has a white van with the same words as his jacket written on the side.

OUT OF THE WILD.

Steve throws Dawn's bag in the back of the van. Then he turns back to Wendy. "This usually takes about two to three months," he tells her. "Depending on the kid. You need a ride to your hotel?"

Wendy shakes her head. Says something about a shuttle bus.

"Okay." Steve shakes her hand again. "We'll be in touch."

Dawn's wondering if she's still high or just half-asleep. Can't process what's happening. Then Wendy's hugging her. Telling her she loves her.

She can't look Dawn in the eyes.

Then Wendy's walking away and Steve's opening the passenger door of the van and he's gesturing to Dawn to get in.

"It's just you and me, kid," he tells Dawn. "Your mom ain't coming back."

Dawn doesn't run.

She *thinks* about running, but where would she go? She's

in *Seattle*, for God's sake. And even her mom wants nothing to do with her.

Anyway, Dawn's maybe a little bit curious. So far, nobody's told her shit.

She gets in the van with Steve.

It's a mistake.